The
Emperor
and the Maula

The Emperor and the Maula

ROBERT SILVERBERG

SUBTERRANEAN PRESS 2017

Signed, Limited Edition

ISBN
978-1-59606-845-2

Subterranean Press
PO Box 190106
Burton, MI 48519

subterraneanpress.com

Table of
Contents

7—INTRODUCTION

15—THE EMPEROR
    AND THE MAULA

Introduction

"WHAT ABOUT a space opera starring Scheherazade?" Byron Preiss asked. He named a very generous fee. *Very* generous.

"Well, why not?" I said, after perhaps ten seconds of earnest deliberation.

The year was 1992. My financial situation just then was, for me, uncharacteristically precarious as a result of a very expensive divorce, and Byron was a very persuasive talker. We had been working together on various projects for fifteen years or so, by then: he ran a small publishing company, specializing in elegantly illustrated books centered in the area of science fiction, fantasy, and popular culture in general, and also packaged books of similar types for larger companies. I had written stories for anthologies he was publishing, I had edited anthologies for him myself, and I had been involved in various peripheral ways in all sorts of Preiss enterprises too numerous to describe here. He was charming, suave, well educated, a splendid friend to have. He was also an astonishingly reckless businessman, who ran his multifarious projects in the most chaotic way, one that was very much the antithesis of my own practices. But I forgave him again and again for that, patiently leading him through explanations of the details that he was so blithely allowing to escape him, and almost always we were able to come to an agreement on terms I could live with.

He sent me a prospectus for the Scheherazade project, which would be called *3001: Millennial Stars*. It was going to be constructed of three 30,000-word novellas, the first of which to be written by me in the next nine months, the other two to be the work of two writers not yet chosen. The plot would center around a young woman—the Scheherazade figure of his telephone call—who boldly ventures from the Earth of A.D. 3001 to the distant capital world of the vast Galactic Empire to persuade the omnipotent ruler of that empire to grant liberty to Earth, which the Empire has incorporated into its territory. To the inhabitants of what is known as Imperial Space, the conquered peoples of Territorial Space are regarded as *maulas*—barbarians—and it is forbidden, on pain of death, for any *maula* to enter into Imperial Space. Our young woman knows that she is risking her life by doing so, but, nevertheless, she intends to smuggle herself into the Imperial capital and put her case before the Emperor himself.

She is, of course, immediately apprehended and sentenced to death, in accordance with Imperial law. But no governmental machinery exists for performing actual executions, and while the Imperial bureaucrats dither over what to do, word of her presence on the capital world drifts upward to the Emperor, who becomes interested in her case and asks to meet her.

The Emperor and the Maula

Immediately taking some interest in her, he asks her to tell him the story of her bold and indeed suicidal mission, warning her to keep it short because she must be delivered to the executioner the following morning.

So we have the underlying structure of the book: a variation on the original Scheherazade concept of the *Thousand Nights and a Night*, for, as I observed to Byron in a letter dated September 17, 1992, "The outline as presented to me called for a Scheherazade format, but whereas Scheherazade was telling *other people's* stories [Sinbad, Aladdin, etc.] to the King, the prospectus requires that Laylah tell *her own* story." And because what I was being asked to write was essentially the first third of a single novel to be written by three different hands, I would have to leave the story incomplete at the end of 30,000 words. The original Scheherazade cunningly leaves each night's story unfinished as dawn arrives, so that the King, caught up in the tale's suspense, allows her to live the next day to finish it; and, of course, whenever she finishes a story she immediately begins a new one, thus postponing the morning of her execution for a thousand nights and a night, until the King, smitten by now by love, not only pardons her but makes her his wife. I would follow the same scheme, my protagonist Laylah drawing things out to fend off her execution until the Emperor, like the King of the old stories, finds himself unable to take her life.

Very well. I wrote my story. Laylah travels to the Imperial capital, goes before the Emperor, tells him the tale of how her beloved native planet was ruthlessly conquered by the Imperial forces. When I reached the 30,000-word mark I broke things off, ending on a cliff-hanger. The King tells Laylah that she must finish her story that evening. Yes, she says. "I will do my best, Majesty. Though it costs me my life, and I know that it will, tonight will see the last of my story." And to herself she says, gloatingly, *I have him! He's caught good and proper, that much is certain! And he will sit and listen to me—and sit—and listen—as long as I want him to—as long as I need him to—* And there I ended it, leaving the plot unresolved in true Scheherazade fashion. At the end of the manuscript I added a note for my successors in the series, headed "For Those Who Follow After" and providing some plot suggestions, though even those ended on an uncertain note:

"But will the Emperor marry her? Or will he, once she has ceased to hold his interest, be forced to send her to the executioner as custom demands? And does she *want* to be part of the royal harem? Perhaps her brother, determined to root out the conspiracy, places new pressures on her. Or her sister turns up somewhere..."

Byron wasn't happy. He complained about the open-endedness of what I had turned in. To which I replied, "I think I did exactly what was asked of me, and though it would have been nice if I could follow the design of the prospectus, which called for a unified ongoing story written by three different people, and still come up with a totally self-contained novella, to do that would have verged on the miraculous. What I did instead was set things up for the writers to come, as I promised to do. Expert professional work is what I specialize in; for miracles I need requests in advance." I ended him by asking him to "take another look at the prospectus you gave me before raising the stand-alone issue."

He took another look, saw that I had a point, and accepted my novella as it stood. In the fullness of time—five months later, in fact; Byron was never one to pay big checks hastily—I got my fee, and that was the last I heard of the project. I asked him, eventually, how the second and third writers were coming along with their stories, since I was mildly curious about how they were going to wind up the plot I had set in motion, and he told me that he was having a little trouble, actually, in finding the other two writers. Well, that wasn't my problem. I had done my part of the job, I had been paid very nicely for it, and I had other projects to think about. I forgot completely about my futuristic Scheherazade. Sooner or later, I assumed, the other two stories would be written and I would get a copy of the finished book, but until then it was no concern of mine.

Now we jump forward more than a decade. In the summer of 2005, Byron was killed in a highway accident. His publishing company, which had been held together by scotch tape and paper clips, turned out to have been a sort of Ponzi scheme, requiring him constantly to come up with new book deals in order to pay the money owed to writers, artists, printers, and distributors for the previous ones. With Byron no longer there to dream up a steady flow of ingenious new proposals, the creditors closed in and his company went into bankruptcy. I suppose the exiting third of the *Millennial Stars* book was one of the assets sold in the bankruptcy sale, but a fragment of a book is of no use to anyone, and I have never heard anything about it from the new owners of his properties.

Indeed the story had long since gone out of my mind. A 30,000-word story was almost impossible to sell anywhere; it was too long to fit in one issue of a magazine, too short to serialize, and most book publishers would regard it as unsuitable at that length for book publication, Besides, my story ended in mid-air, coming to halt without any resolution.

But the appalling shock of Byron's death set me to thinking of all the projects I had done with him, among them "The Emperor and the Maula." Just then, Gardner Dozois and Jonathan Strahan, two editors who are also good friends of mine, were putting together an anthology called *The New Space Opera* for Harper & Row, and they asked me for a story. Well, there was "The Emperor and the Maula," sitting in a dusty corner of my computer. But there were two problems. The story was unfinished; and it was 30,000 words long, exactly twice as long as the maximum word limit for the Dozois-Strahan book.

But I am resourceful, am I not? I am a cagy old pro, is that not so? And I am a thrifty guy who hates to waste an unpublished story. Publishing rights to my Scheherazade novella had never been used, and I knew they never would be. So I tell my pals Jonathan and Gardner that I have just the thing for them, and I set out to cut my old novella in half and supply a real ending for it.

Finding an ending turns out to be the lesser task. Picking up where I had left off in 1992, I write a new final scene in which Laylah and the Emperor circle each other until they both have achieved what they want from each other, after which I provide a snappy final paragraph that continues the *Thousand Nights and a Night* parallel without leaving the reader unsatisfied. Doing that took just a single morning. Cutting the story down from 30,000 words to 15,000, though, was a truly onerous headache. Some minor scenes could be dispensed with entirely, but I still needed to maintain the structure of what had once been a 120-page manuscript that now would run just 60 pages. I stripped away great blocks of colorful description. I made conversations much more terse while nonetheless keeping the plot purpose of each scene intact. I chopped and I chopped and I chopped, and somehow got the story down to the required length, feeling sad about all that I had thrown out but still confident that the drastically abridged story made narrative sense.

I sent it to Gardner and Jonathan, who accepted it quickly and happily, and it appeared in 2007 in their fine fat *New Space Opera* anthology, cheek by jowl with stories by Nancy Kress, Ian McDonald, Gregory Benford, Dan Simmons, and a lot of other top-drawer writers. And for a second time it went out of my mind. I had been paid twice for it, and very well, too, after all, and it had finally been published, and that was that. Until, in the summer of 2016, I was afflicted with some computer trouble, and in the course of cleaning things up I discovered that the original unabridged version of *The Emperor and the Maula* was still lurking in that dusty corner of my hard disk. In great curiosity I began to read it, and discovered that it was, actually, altogether different in tone from the version Dozois and Strahan had published a decade before. Whereas the stripped-down version moved with the zip and zap that a space-opera novelet ought to have, the unabridged text was leisurely, discursive, pausing here and there to make some little point or to splash in a bit of color that I had

had to dispense with during the editing task. It was, I decided, deserving of publication in its own right.

And so here it is. Not ending in mid-air as I had originally left it, however, since that (in the absence of the intended pair of novellas that had been supposed to finish the story) would leave everybody unsatisfied. So I borrowed the new ending that I had written for the Dozois-Strahan anthology and grafted it onto the former final scene of the novella. It is, for me, a satisfactory resolution, and so it is for Laylah and the Emperor, too, and, I hope, also for my readers.

—Robert Silverberg, November, 2016

The Emperor and the Maula

Bogan 17, 82nd Dynastic Cycle
(August 3, A.D. 3001)

T HE GONGS have sounded throughout the ship. We have
crossed the invisible line that separates Territorial Space from
Imperial Space and I am still aboard; so now my life is officially forfeit. Not that anyone on the ship seems to care. It's no
business of theirs, after all. The responsibility for knowing and
obeying the tiihad—the social code of the Empire—is, so far as I
understand it, and I hope that I do, something that each individual citizen must look after for himself. Or herself, or itself.

And I have chosen to break that code. So be it. My life is forfeit now—or will be, when we land on Capital World.

We'll see about that when we land.

Meanwhile here I am—an Earthborn woman, a mere barbaric maula, getting deeper into Imperial Space with each passing
light-second. I should be trembling with fear, I suppose.

No.

Let the Emperor tremble. Laylah is here!

—From the Diaries of Laylah Walis

▷▷ 1.

IT WAS a highly unusual case. No one at the Capital World starport had ever confronted anything like it before, and no one had the slightest idea of how to deal with it. Which is how it happened to reach the attention, finally, of no less a personage than the Emperor Ryah VII himself, the High Ansaar, the Supreme Omniscience, the Most Holy Defender of the Race.

The chain that led ultimately to the Emperor began with a certain Loompan Chilidor, an arbiter of passenger manifests at the Capital starport. Loompan Chilidor was a short-crested, pale-skinned, insignificant low-caste person whose simple low-caste job it was to hold up a neural scanner while the passengers of a newly arrived starship disembarked. As they moved across the landing apron and into the cloud of purple luminance that was the scanner field, each passenger's identity was registered, checked against the records of the Imperial Transit Authority, and noted in the archives under the proper planet of origin.

That was all there was to it. The myriad citizens of the Ansaar Empire enjoyed great freedom of travel, moving as they wished from world to world and from star-system to star-system with a minimum of bureaucratic interference, and the purpose of Loompan Chilidor's job was merely to provide statistical data on the patterns of travel flow within the Empire.

But something quite unexpected occurred as he was running the routine transit check on the travelers who had just arrived from the Seppuldidorior system aboard the starship Velipok. About half the Velipok's passengers had shuffled uneventfully through the luminance field and on into the waiting ground-transportation pods when suddenly jagged incandescent streaks of vivid green burst forth on the purple surface of the field.

Tiihad violation!

That was the highest of the six levels of irregularity that the scanner field was designed to detect—higher even than vribor, which was the carrying of infectious disease, and gulimil, the smuggling of dangerous weapons, and shhtek, the open wearing of medallions of the extinct and proscribed Simgoin Dynasty. Violation of tiihad was an assault on the fundamental societal structure of the Empire itself.

Loompan Chilidor's long dangling arms jerked in shock. His small yellow eyes took on the orange tinge of hormonal response to surprise and stress. From the depths of his throat came a guttural moan of dismay.

His training, though, carried him swiftly through his part in the crisis. The thing he was supposed to do, in the unlikely event of a scanner alarm, was to press the red button that he wore on the breast of his uniform. That would automatically seal the luminance field, preventing the escape of the culprit, and simultaneously would bring the problem to the attention of his immediate superior, Domtel Tribuso, Manager of Passenger Flow.

Loompan Chilidor pressed his button. That concluded Loompan Chilidor's role in the event.

Domtel Tribuso, who was stocky and slow, appeared in due course from his office in the terminal building. The purple luminance field had by now become a rubbery-walled purple cage. Three or four dozen newly arrived travelers were trapped inside, gesticulating angrily at the Manager of Passenger Flow through its translucent walls. Some time had passed since Loompan Chilidor had pressed his button and no doubt the atmosphere inside the cage had grown less than pleasant.

Domtel Tribuso stared in puzzlement and some annoyance at the jagged green streaks that crisscrossed the outer surface of the field.

"Green?" the Manager of Passenger Flow said. "That's a tiihad violation, isn't it?" He peered through the walls of the cage.

There was a maula in there.

Most of the passengers, Domtel Tribuso saw at once, were Ansaar. It was improbable that they could be the source of the trouble. Any Ansaar arriving on holy Haraar, whether resident or visitor, would know what kind of behavior was expected here. There were a few Liigachi and a pair of Vrulvruls and a cluster of agitated-looking Zmachs, too, but Liigachi and Vrulvruls and Zmachs had held full citizenship in the Imperium for many centuries, and surely understood the usages of proper decorum.

One of the passengers, though, was a creature such as Domtel Tribuso could not identify at all. An alien, yes, certainly: but a non-Imperial alien, an inferior barbaric life-form from the Territories, a trespasser and transgressor here on this hallowed world. A maula. Domtel Tribuso felt amazement and disgust and anger.

The maula was tall, and slender to the point of gauntness, and its face was as flat as a platter, with all the features set close together in the middle, its eyes practically next to each other, its nose a tiny button just below, its mouth—Domtel Tribuso supposed that that was a mouth—a mere slit near its chin. Its legs were much too long for its body and its arms grotesquely short. The creature had no crest, only a short crop of unpleasant dark fur sprouting from its skull. There were two strange round swellings on its chest, about the size of fists.

Hideous. Hideous. And what was it doing here, on Haraar, of all worlds of the Empire?

The Manager of Passenger Flow summoned his aides.

"Get that maula out of there and bring it to Examination Chamber Three. Offer apologies to the other passengers and send them on their way as fast as you can."

Examination Chamber Three was the holding cell where unauthorized life-forms were investigated. Domtel Tribuso could not remember a time when it had been used for anything more challenging than the inspection of unfamiliar pets or trophy-animals that some citizen of the Imperium had acquired in the course of travel in some rarely visited region of Territorial Space, and which needed to be checked by an Imperial veterinarian before being released from starport quarantine.

The Emperor and the Maula

But this creature was no pet or trophy, this maula, and it did not appear to belong to any of the other passengers. Plainly it was an intelligent life-form—a properly ticketed passenger in its own right, apparently. It was standing quite calmly in the group of newly disembarked passengers of Citizen rank as though it regarded itself as one of them. It was even carrying several pieces of expensive-looking hand-luggage.

Domtel Tribuso did not understand how a maula had been able to purchase a ticket to Haraar or any other world within Imperial Space, or why the ground personnel at the point of embarkation had allowed it to go on board the Velipok, or why the Velipok's captain had not called ahead by subradio to Haraar to let it be known that there was a maula on board. Those things would need to be investigated, Domtel Tribuso knew.

But not by him. This affair—this scandal; that was the only word for it, really—had already gone beyond his level of responsibility. He summoned his superior, Graligal Dren, who had jurisdiction over passport irregularities, and turned the maula over to her.

Graligal Dren, a mid-caste woman of a rich olive hue with a high-peaked sagittal crest of admirable narrowness and delicacy, had completed a full decade in her position without any kind of reprimand or censure. Two more spotless years would entitle her to the medallion of the Order of the Dynasty. She wasn't amused to have a nasty complication like this cropping up now.

Glowering through the thick glass wall that separated her from the maula, she said, "Are you able to understand Universal Imperial, creature?"

"I speak it quite well, thank you," the maula replied, in a clear, high-pitched voice, with a slight hint of a West Quadrant accent.

"Good. And do you have a name?"

"My name is Laylah Walis."

An incomprehensible gargling noise, mere sounds. Which of them was the soul-name, which was the face-name? Foolish to wonder about such things in the case of a maula, Graligal Dren thought. One should expect barbarians to have barbaric names. And there the name was, all right, smack in the middle of the passenger manifest: LAYLAH WALIS. The emigration people who had allowed it to board a Haraar-bound ship must have been out of their minds.

"Your planet of embarkation was Hathpoin in the Seppuldidorior system?"

"That's correct."

"But you're no Seppuldidoriori. Where did you come from before that?"

"Mingtha, in the Ghair system. Which I reached by way of Zemblano, which is in Briff. And before that—"

"Don't give me your whole itinerary, creature. Just tell me where you are from originally."

"Earth," the maula said.

"Earth? Never heard of it."

"It's a small world in what you would call the Northwest Arm. The third planet of a sun called Sol. It's been part of the Empire for about twenty years now."

"The Northwest Arm," Graligal Dren repeated. The image came to her mind of a zone of wild scruffy worlds inhabited by shambling bestial creatures—frontier worlds, barely civilized, dismal primitive outposts of the Empire valuable only for the raw materials they had to offer. It amazed her that a creature from a world such as that could speak Universal Imperial with such precision and force; and with such haughtiness, too. You would think that this maula had twenty generations of Dynastic blood in its veins. And, of course, during the entire conversation it had made not the slightest attempt to assume a posture of respect, though Graligal Dren was plainly an individual of relatively distinguished caste. It was simply staring at her in its ugly flat-faced way. What arrogance! What foolishness! But only an arrogant fool of a maula would have attempted to come to Haraar. "Tell me, Laylah Walis," said Graligal Dren, "are you aware of where you are now?"

"Of course. This is Haraar, the Capital World, the seat of the Imperial Government."

"Yes. The home world of the Ansaaran race. The heart and soul of the Empire."

"Exactly."

"You came here, then, in full consciousness of what you were doing?"

"Of course."

"Knowing that it is forbidden under pain of the most severe penalties for Territorials to enter any part of Imperial Space without special permission, and in particular to come here, under any circumstances at all?"

"Yes."

"The most severe penalties," Graligal Dren said again. "Most severe."

"I was quite aware of that, yes."

This was madness. Graligal Dren began to feel a little sick to her stomach.

It seemed necessary to change the subject. "How were you able to obtain a ticket?" she asked.

"It's a long story," the maula said. "But basically I told someone who was in a position to get one for me that I wanted to visit Haraar, and he arranged it for me."

"And no one tried to prevent you from boarding the ship at Hathpoin Starport?"

"Obviously not."

Graligal Dren made a steeple of her fingers and interlaced both sets of her thumbs. This maula seemed incredibly sure of itself: a kind of lunatic self-confidence. But how much did it really know of Ansaar laws and customs?

"This world is sacred ground," Graligal Dren said slowly. "It is the fount and origin of our race. We revere the very dust that blows through its humblest alleyways. You must understand that we have never allowed this holy world to be desecrated by creatures who are—whom we regard as—who can be defined as—"

"Maulas," said Laylah Walis. "Barbarians. Inherently inferior beings."

"Exactly."

"And you maintain the purity of your holy world," the maula said, "by inflicting a penalty of death on any maula who dares to set foot here."

Graligal Dren stared.

"So you did know that before you came here?" she said, finally.

"Absolutely."

"And you came here anyway?"

"It certainly would seem that way," said Laylah Walis.

$\gg$ 2.

T WAS much too much for Graligal Dren to handle. If suicide was what this unfortunate creature intended to commit, the maula was going to have to do it without the help of Graligal Dren.

She passed the case along then and there to her superior, Viban Thoth, Director of Immigration Facilities. Viban Thoth, after a brief and discomforting study of the file thus far, quickly determined that this was a matter for Starport Security. He sent the file up there.

Commissioner Twimat Dulik of Security, a short burly man who was not one for letting unfinished business clutter his desk, swiftly carried out his own interrogation of the prisoner and confirmed that it was a Territorial creature, a native of one of the newly conquered worlds in the West Quadrant—a mammalian being of the sort that called themselves "humans." Although this particular being appeared intelligent enough, in its way, it unquestionably belonged to a species that was technically classed as maula: sub-civilized, officially unclean, contemptible by definition.

And, of course, it was strictly forbidden for maulas to desecrate the Capital World by their presence. By coming to Haraar, the maula had automatically made itself subject to a penalty of death, without even the necessity of a formal trial.

The damnable thing was that the maula seemed to understand all that, and didn't appear to care in the least.

Which made no sense to Commissioner Twimat Dulik.

"Since the maula is aware of the penalty for its violation of tiihad, and chose to trespass here anyway, the maula is obviously insane," said Commissioner Twimat Dulik to his own immediate superior, Justiciar Hwillinin Ma of the Department of Criminal Affairs. "We are supposed to be civilized beings. Do we have the right to subject an insane person to the death penalty?"

Justiciar Hwillinin Ma, a mid-upper-caste neuter with dusky yellow skin and a lengthy crest that was, unfortunately, of very low contour, gave Commissioner Twimat Dulik a dark irritable look and said, "A maula is not a person, Dulik. A maula is scarcely anything more than a brute animal. That is point one. Point two is that our legal definitions of insanity can't be applied to sub-civilized beings, any more than they could be to insects or birds or trees. Point three—"

"This isn't an insect or a bird or a tree, Justiciar Ma. This is an alert, seemingly intelligent creature who speaks Universal Imperial as well as any—"

"Point three," said Justiciar Hwillinin Ma sternly, "is that the law is quite explicit on the subject of maula desecration of the home world. The penalty is death. There's no footnote covering sanity or insanity. Or the quality of one's command of Universal Imperial. The home world must be protected against desecration and the traditional act of purification is the immediate slaying of the desecrator."

Commissioner Twimat Dulik nodded.

"Very well, then, Justiciar Ma. I've had the ruling I came here for. In my capacity as Commissioner of Starport Security I herewith turn the maula prisoner Laylah Walis that we have apprehended over to you for execution of the prescribed penalty. Good day to you, Justiciar Ma."

The Commissioner saluted and went out.

Very well, thought Justiciar Ma: there was no disputing what Dulik had said. His task now was to move the unexpected problem along to a swift and proper solution.

Justiciar Ma nudged the transmission node of his desk communicator.

"The maula Laylah Walis is found guilty of high trespass and desecration, and is remanded to the Haraar City Department of Criminal Justice for execution," he said crisply. And dismissed the case from his mind.

But the Haraar City Department of Criminal Justice, Justiciar Ma learned to his displeasure ten minutes later, would not accept the prisoner. The departmental subaltern whose responsibility it was to turn the maula over to the city police had made the mistake of phoning them first to pass along the news that a maula had been taken into custody at the starport and that the prisoner was now about to be sent on its way to them, by order of Justiciar

Hwillinin Ma, so that it could be put to death for its reckless violation of tiihad.

"Oh, no," said the chief aide to the Prefect of Capital Police. "You can't ship any maulas into town, fellow! Don't you realize that that only compounds the desecration?"

"But Justiciar Ma says—"

"Justiciar Ma can gedoy his gevasht," the chief aide to the Prefect of Capital Police replied calmly. "It's bad enough that this maula of yours is polluting the starport, but do you seriously think that we're going to allow it to be brought into the capital city itself? That we would let it get within a hundred glezzans of the High Temple precincts? Let alone anywhere near the Imperial Palace? Do you realize that the Emperor is in residence this very minute? He can smell a maula from five glezzans away. Oh, no, no, no. You keep your maula in your own jurisdiction, please, and don't try to foul the holy city with it."

"But a death penalty needs to be carried out—"

"You've got weapons somewhere around the starport, don't you? If the maula is supposed to be put to death, that's your problem, not ours. Just take it out behind a fuel dump somewhere back of the terminal and blow its head off. There's nothing to it, really. As long as you remember to point your blaster in the right direction. The long end goes toward the prisoner."

The chief aide to the Prefect of Capital Police laughed.

And the screen went blank.

"The police won't accept the maula," the subaltern glumly reported to Justiciar Ma.

"But the execution—"

"They say we have to do it."

Justiciar Ma stared. "We do?"

"Yes, sir."

The Justiciar closed his eyes and drew a deep breath. After a moment he said, "All right, then. Go over to the holding cell and take care of it right away. And be sure you follow the prescribed procedures, whatever they may happen to be."

"Me, sir?" the subaltern said, in a throttled tone of high incredulity.

"You, yes. Who do you think I'm talking to?"

"Execute the maula myself, sir?"

Justiciar Ma stared stonily in the subaltern's direction and said nothing.

"Sir? Sir? Sir?"

▷▷ 3.

UT IT was one thing, Justiciar Ma soon discovered, to issue an execution order, and another thing entirely to get it carried out. In the end, he was unable to find anyone at the starport who could be induced to put the maula to death.

It was true enough that the maula had committed a heinous misdeed and that the law called for its immediate execution. But it wasn't as though such violations were an everyday event at the Capital World starport. In fact, nobody could remember the last time a maula had actually been caught trying to land on Haraar.

A hasty search of the archives eventually revealed that the most recent such case had taken place during the 80th Dynastic Cycle, some 641 years previously. So the maula's transgression, deplorable though it was, seemed to be a crime of the sort which everyone regarded with high indignation but which in fact very rarely was ever committed. And in any case there didn't happen to be any executioners among the official personnel of the star-port. Arbiters of this and that, yes, and managers of this and that, and inspectors of this and that, and commissioners of this and that, and even one Justiciar. But no one at all whose regular official duties included the carrying out of executions.

"The law clearly states that a maula caught anywhere on Haraar must be killed immediately," Justiciar Ma said. He was speaking to his old university classmate Thrippel Vree, who was a Third Chamberlain to His Imperial Majesty. "We've already had it in an examination chamber here for something like fourteen hours. Nobody wants to do the job, and I don't seem to have the legal right to compel anyone to do it. Meanwhile we're all becoming accessories to the desecration."

"You could always kill it yourself," Thrippel Vree suggested blandly.

"Myself?"

"You're the highest-ranking member of the Criminal Affairs Department on the premises, aren't you? So the responsibility ultimately is yours. And if you can't find anyone else who's willing to do it—"

"I can't kill someone, Thrippel!"

"Why not? What did you go into the Criminal Affairs Department for, if not for the pleasure of seeing to it that the laws are respected? And if the law calls for a death penalty—"

"But not with my own hands!"

"And if there's an investigation, and it comes to light that you failed to take the appropriate measures—?"

"Be reasonable," Justiciar Ma moaned.

"One quick shot with a blaster would do it. Deep breath, steady hand, ready, aim, fire. Stuff the body in the fusion converters. File your report. Justice is done."

"No. No. No. No!"

"Well, then—"

Justiciar Ma knew that his old friend was merely being playful. Surely Vree couldn't be serious. Surely.

And yet—why not do it himself?

No. No. No.

He simply couldn't. It was beneath his dignity. He was a Justiciar, not an executioner. And besides—to kill someone— even a prisoner—even a maula who had desecrated the holy planet of Haraar—

No.

It wasn't that Justiciar Ma was particularly merciful, nor especially soft-hearted. The Ansaar were not a race noted for mercy or soft-heartedness: one did not get to control three fifths of the known galaxy by being extraordinarily merciful or tender. But conquering entire solar systems for the greater glory of the Empire was one thing and taking some hapless sub-civilized creature out back and shooting it in cold blood was another. Especially when you happened to be a middle-aged bureaucrat of fairly high caste and sedentary nature.

Let those whose profession it is to execute people do the executing, Justiciar Ma thought.

But there were no executioners to be had around the starport, and no way to convey the prisoner to a place where executioners might be available.

Justiciar Ma continued to stew over his problem for twelve hours more, growing steadily more convinced that ultimately he was going to pay with his career for the damnable impertinence of this confounded maula. A couple of times during those dreary twelve hours he came almost to the verge of carrying out the execution personally, despite all his hesitations, purely to save his own neck.

But meanwhile Third Chamberlain Thrippel Vree managed to save it for him.

What happened was that Third Chamberlain Vree chanced to mention the starport episode, somewhat later that evening, to another Third Chamberlain—there were a hundred and one officials of that rank at His Majesty's court—named Danol Giyango. "How perplexing," said Danol Giyango. "The creature must have known it would have to die for its audacity. And yet it made the voyage anyway. What could it possibly have expected to gain?"

The paradox was so intriguing that Danol Giyango spoke of it to his wife, who was a Lady-in-Waiting, who made mention of it after dinner to one of the High Eunuchs of the Innermost Chamber, who told a Subsidiary Concubine, who happened to be in attendance later that night on one of the five Cherished Major Wives, Etaag Thuuyaal. And that night was Etaag Thuuyaal's turn to spend with His Majesty the Emperor Ryah VII, the High Ansaar, the Supreme Omniscience, the Most Holy Defender of the Race.

"I heard the most extraordinary story a little while ago," said Etaag Thuuyaal to the Emperor, as they lay amiably entwined in the Imperial hammock very much later that night. The Emperor, she knew—as who did not?—was a connoisseur of extraordinary stories, with a voracious appetite for the unlikely and the divertingly strange, a man of intense curiosities and powerful whims.

"And what might that be, my dearest one?" he asked, gently stroking her sleek pale back.

"Well," said Etaag Thuuyal, "this comes from Subsidiary Concubine Hypoepoi, who heard it from the High Eunuch Sambin, who got it from Lady-in-Waiting Sipyar Giyango, whose husband heard it from somebody whose friend is a Justiciar at the starport. It seems that a starship arrived this morning from someplace out in the Territories, and when the passengers disembarked it was discovered that one of them was—can you imagine it?—no, you would never guess, not in a million years—well, the passengers came down the ramp, and most of them were the usual assortment of tourists and pilgrims and such, but then what do you think marched out of the ship, as blithe and bold as anything could be—?"

"Tell me," said the Emperor Ryah VII.

Etaag Thuuyal smiled with deep self-satisfaction. Great benefits, she had learned long ago, accrued to those who were capable of keeping the Emperor amused.

"Well," she said, "what I heard was—"

And at last she unrolled the story as it had traveled up the chain of communication to her ears.

The Emperor was startled. And fascinated as well.

A maula on Haraar? Well, of course, the creature would have to die. An offense of that magnitude couldn't go unpunished. Propriety demanded it.

But—all proprieties aside—the Emperor Ryah VII was instantly taken by the inherent mystery of the maula's apparently suicidal decision to travel to the Capital World by commercial spaceliner in full knowledge of the risk involved. Suicide, he knew, was not a typical behavior pattern of barbarians and other simple life-forms. They might be uneducated and coarse and dull-witted and crude, but never were they blind to their own survival imperatives. Like all primitive animals, they burned within with the furious species-need to live and reproduce and maintain their species' niche in the great chain of being. An animal might gnaw off its own leg in order to escape from a trap into which it had stumbled, the Emperor thought, but it was hardly likely to stick its leg in the trap in the first place, purely to find out if the trap really would close on it.

So why—why—

"There must be an explanation for what this maula has done. To march with open eyes into certain death—no, no, it must have had a reason that made sense to it," said the Emperor. "It must have. What possibly could have possessed the creature? I have to find out!" His face was aglow with excitement. He sprang lithely out of the hammock and called for the eunuch on duty.

"A maula has turned up at the starport aboard a liner from Seppuldidorior and it seems they haven't executed it yet. Find out if that's so. And if the execution really hasn't take place, tell them that I've ordered a day's delay in the carrying out of the sentence. I want to talk to this maula first. Have it brought here first thing in the morning."

"I hear and obey, O Lord of the Universe."

"Run along, then."

The Emperor returned to his hammock. Etaag Thuuyal stretched out her arms to him, amiably, invitingly.

⤏ 4.

AYLAH WALIS was beginning to worry—just a little. Or perhaps more than a little; but she tried to keep her uneasiness under control. Everything so far had gone pretty much according to plan, after all. She had actually managed to get to Haraar, which was no easy trick for someone from the Territories. And she had survived the critical first few hours of her presence here without suffering the fate of summary execution to which, at least in theory, she could have been subjected.

But now—

Now she was in jail, more or less, and the hours were ticking along—it must be almost dawn by now—and she wasn't at all sure what was going to happen next. The fact that a whole series of Imperial bureaucrats had come to interrogate her during the course of the day, each obviously holding a higher rank in the official hierarchy than the one before, was a good sign. The more of them who came, the better. Especially since the more highly placed ones had appeared distinctly intrigued and perplexed by the inexplicable fact of her arrival here.

The biggest risk had been that some clod of a low-caste port functionary, aware of the stringent desecration law and devoid of all curiosity about why Laylah might have chosen to violate it, would simply haul out his blaster and impose the appropriate sentence on her the moment she stepped off the starship. But that hadn't happened; and now she had put her hooks in some bigger fish. If her calculations were correct, the mystifying tale of the maula at the starport was continuing to climb up and up in the hierarchical levels, until eventually it would come to the ear of the Emperor himself. And then—

Then—

But that was if her calculations were correct. It was all a wild gamble, a thousand-to-one shot, and she had known it from the start. A much more likely outcome would be that the port officials, after dithering around for a day or so, would finally come to the conclusion that the decree concerning desecration of the Capital World by maulas meant exactly what it seemed to mean, and that they had no choice but to invoke a sentence of summary execution. And then, as soon as they had shuffled through the proper bureaucratic procedures, the door of her holding chamber would open and some grim masked functionary would step inside and—

She could hear sounds in the hall. People approaching, right on cue.

Then through the glass window of her cell Laylah saw three figures. One was the stocky little security chief, Dulik, who had spoken with her earlier that day. He had seemed intelligent and sensitive, even sympathetic. The other two, who flanked him at what Laylah knew was the proper distance of respect in this culture of elaborate social distinctions, were brutish-looking low-caste Ansaar in somber dull-green uniforms, even shorter and more chunky than Dulik—some sort of security guards, she supposed.

Executioners?

Certainly they looked grim, all three of them. Laylah had made a careful study over the course of many years of Ansaar body language, and the posture of these three, as she surveyed them through the window, seemed ominous indeed. They held themselves very stiffly, shoulders pushed up practically to their ears and long arms close to their sides, and their eyes were retracted in their sockets, always a mark of tension among the Ansaar, with the vertical slits of their pupils nearly invisible.

The cell door swung open.

"You are summoned, Laylah Walis," the security chief said, in a taut and portentous tone.

He seemed almost to be trembling.

Were they going to execute her on the spot, then? Laylah's studies in modern Ansaar culture had told her that the death penalty, though it was prescribed for all manner of breaches of taboo, was very rarely inflicted nowadays, at least on the inner worlds of the Imperium, and it was generally regarded by most citizens as a harsh and unsavory relic of an earlier and more violent era. Now that the Ansaar had conquered as much of the galaxy as they seemed to require, they were mellowing, evidently, into a more easy-going race. Which might explain why these three looked so tense and miserable, if indeed they found themselves with no choice but to put their prisoner to death right here and now for her defiance of the tiihad rules.

"Summoned to what?" she said, as calmly as she could.

"Not to what, maula, but to whom. The Emperor has requested that you be brought to him. For some reason he is interested in speaking with you before you die."

The Emperor?

Then it had all worked out the right way, after all! Laylah allowed a quick smile to flit across her face. A surge of relief flooded through her. Success! Success! Not an execution, but an audience with the High Ansaar himself!

But then one of the two low-caste Ansaar produced a coil of rope from a sack that he was carrying and the other grabbed her arms and yanked them roughly behind her back as though she were a beast being trussed for slaughter.

"Hey! What are you doing?"

"It would be worth our heads if you were somehow to escape," said the security chief, as the guards proceeded to tie her wrists tightly together, and then her ankles. "We intend to take no chances whatever with you." He signalled to the guards, who seized her by the elbows and propelled her across the room and out the door of the cell.

It was awkward and humiliating. She was a head and a half taller than the two Ansaar and it was all they could do to hold her upright. Her legs dragged behind her as they pulled her clumsily along, and their sharp-clawed seven-fingered hands dug miserably into her flesh as they sought to maintain their grip on her. All she could do was to relax her body as much as possible and try to make things easy for them. But even so she felt stretched and bruised and cramped by the time they had hauled her in a series of bumps and jolts down an interminable tunnel and out into the bright golden-green light of the Haraar dawn.

A sleek teardrop-shaped car was waiting. They dumped her inside, and jumped in alongside her.

"The Imperial Palace," she heard Dulik say to the driver. And then, in a muttered undertone: "He delays the maula's death. He must speak with her first, we are told. Well, who are we to question the Emperor's wishes? Who are we, indeed?"

There was a humming sound as the magnetic rotors cut in.

Then the car lifted and floated down the track that would take it out of the starport and toward Haraar City, the fabled capital of the Ansaar Empire.

Tales of the beauty and splendor of the great Ansaar metropolis were told everywhere in the known galaxy. "The rose-red city half as old as time," a poet had called it—a city of a thousand palaces and five thousand temples, of green parks and leafy promenades, of shining stone obelisks and long eye-dazzling colonnades. From here, the invincible imperialist might of the Ansaar had radiated relentlessly and irresistibly outward over the past ninety thousand years, spreading and spreading from planet to planet and from system to system in ever-widening circles until the Ansaar host controlled a dominion that arched across better than a thousand parsecs of space. And for eons the wealth of all that vast empire had poured down in torrents upon this city of Haraar, making it the most majestic seat of government that had ever existed anywhere.

But little of the capital's wondrous beauty was visible to Laylah Walis as the maglev car in which she rode floated silently toward the center of the city. She sat hunched down between the two Ansaar guards, her long legs sprawling far forward and her head uncomfortably buried in a plush cushion; and all she could see at the angle she was forced to assume was a glimpse of a golden dome here, a pink minaret there, a great gleaming black obelisk jutting into the sky over yonder.

The car floated to a halt. Ungently the guards pulled her from it.

She had one astounding glimpse of her surroundings: the courtyard of an incredible palace: high gleaming walls of porphyry inlaid with medallions of onyx rising before her—delicate many-windowed towers of dizzying height climbing far above them—long boulevards lined by strips of immaculately tended shrubbery stretching off to left and right, with crystalline reflecting pools, narrow as daggers, running down their middles—a colossal shining globe of translucent quartz right in front of her through the intricate channels of which flowed rivers of shimmering quicksilver moving in brilliant pulsations—

Then a thick smelly hood of some dense furry fabric was pulled down over Laylah's head and she saw nothing further.

"This is the maula that the Emperor asked us to bring to him," Laylah heard Dulik saying—speaking to palace officials, no doubt. There was an interchange of low muffled words; her hood was lifted for a moment and yellow Ansaar eyes, cat-like and unfriendly, peered briefly into her own, and then the hood descended again; and suddenly she was swept off her feet and carried away, arms and legs dangling unceremoniously in mid-air, with no more care for her comfort than a sack of produce being hauled into a market would have received.

She clamped her lips tight and muttered some angry words within the privacy of her mind. This was hardly the kind of reception she had imagined, when she had first heard that she was to be taken before the Emperor.

But worse was to come.

There was an endless time of footsteps clattering down some marble hall; then the sound of a great door being swung back; and then the bruising impact of being dropped like so much merchandise onto a stone floor.

Laylah lay there, listening to the echoing drumbeat of retreating footsteps, and then to a silence so intense that it roared in her ears.

She was alone, so far as she could tell—bound and hooded, lying on a cold slab of stone in the middle of what must have been an immense empty room. The ropes that encircled her wrists and ankles were beginning to chafe and cut cruelly into her skin, and she felt stifled and nauseated by the increasingly stale, moist air within the hood that covered her face.

She remained that way for hours, struggling for breath, unable to see, and virtually unable to move. She itched in a dozen places and could do nothing about it. Her legs and back grew stiff and sore. She wriggled and twisted, trying to loosen her muscles, but it was all but useless. The stone beneath her body grew colder and colder. Lying on a block of ice could hardly have been more unpleasant. At least ice would melt, after a while. But this stone floor—no doubt it was beautifully polished and magnificent in hue and texture; it might have been the finest marble, or perhaps travertine or alabaster—was devoid of all warmth and miserably unsatisfactory as something to lie on.

Footsteps, finally. Many people approaching.

Voices, growing closer.

The hood being lifted at long last. Laylah blinked, gasped eagerly for breath, scratched her chin against her shoulder to gratify the itch that had begun to plague her half a million years before.

She was indeed in a bleak, enormous stone-walled chamber, high-ceilinged and windowless and altogether bare except for a few small statues set in niches in the distant corners of the room. It might have been a drilling-hall for soldiers. All around her stood a ring of armed guards in comic-opera uniforms: flowing crimson pantaloons, great green sashes, loose purple tunics with great flaring shoulder-pads. Like all the other Ansaar she had seen thus far in her life, they were unprepossessing to behold, short and stocky of build, with thick chests and long ape-like arms and stubby bowed legs.

But standing in front of her, apart from all the others and studying her as though she were some rare and curious zoological specimen, was an Ansaar of such noble mien and grandeur that Laylah knew at once that she must be in the presence of the Emperor Ryah VII.

He seemed to be almost of a different species from the other Ansaar. He was immensely tall, not only for an Ansaar but very likely taller than any human man Laylah had known: well over two meters, she guessed, perhaps two and a half. His proportions were more like those of a human than an Ansaar, too: his legs were long and tapered, and his arms, though of a goodly length, were nothing like the dangling gorilla-arms of the guards, but reached only as far as his thighs, as a human's arms would. The sagittal crest that ornamented his hairless head was the most impressive Ansaar crest she had ever seen, reaching well past his earlobes and extending almost to the small of his neck, and its contours were awesomely steep, rising to needle-sharp prominence—a mark, Laylah knew, of the highest caste.

His skin color, too, was unfamiliar. The Ansaar she had previously seen ranged in hue from the palest tan to a deep olive. From throat to ankles this Ansaar was swathed in a thickly brocaded robe of heavy crimson fabric shot through with threads of silver; but his face and hands were visible, and they were the color of richest mahogany, with a fiery scarlet undertone. Out of that deep-toned mask of a face came the gleam of penetrating green eyes—not yellow, like other Ansaar eyes, but green, the lustrous heavy green of pure emerald.

Surely this was someone who had been bred for a thousand generations for the purpose of occupying the Sapphire Throne of the Ansaar Empire.

He was truly kingly in a way that Laylah had not imagined possible. There was the clear aura of royalty about him from head to toe. Despite herself, despite the profound and fierce loathing for all things Ansaaran that burned within the bosom of every member of the human species, Laylah felt a powerful throb of awe—and an unmistakable, astonishing, incredible shiver of immediate physical attraction.

"Lift it up," the Emperor said, in a voice that rumbled with authority and sonorous force. "Let me see what this maula looks like."

The guards raised her to a standing position. Her legs were cramped and stiff, and she nearly toppled; but she held herself upright with a fierce effort, struggling to ignore the pricklings that shot through her feet and calves like shafts of fire. Lifting her head, she stared directly at him, her eyes meeting his directly, the upper-caste style of Ansaar social usage, her head inclined at precisely the correct angle to indicate deference to his majestic person while retaining her own personal dignity.

"A she-maula, I'd guess. But look at her! Look at her!" the Emperor cried. "Is that a maula expression on her face? Is that the way a maula would stand? She holds herself like a countess! She looks right into my eyes the way a high-caste woman would!" Then he smiled a jagged Ansaar smile and said, "You are a woman, aren't you, maula? I don't know much about humans, actually. But you seem female to me."

"You are completely correct in that assumption, Majesty," said Laylah coolly.

He chuckled. "And she speaks perfect Universal! Just like a lady of the court! Better than some, in fact." The Emperor took a couple of sauntering steps toward her, his vertical pupils narrowing to slits, his brilliant green eyes gleaming brightly with the insatiable curiosity for which he was famed. "What a strange one you are. Where did you learn such good Universal, maula?"

"It's a very long story, O Supreme Omniscience," Laylah replied.

"Ah. Ah. A long story, indeed." He nodded and smiled. He seemed tremendously amused by her. *This is working very well so far,* Laylah thought delightedly. "You must tell it to me, then. In a somewhat shortened version, if you would. Three ambassadors are waiting to see me today, and the Goishlaar of Gozishtandar is here besides. The Goishlaar wants favors from me, as usual, and that always makes him very impatient."

She was silent.

"Go on," said Ryah, after a moment. "I asked you to speak. Tell me about yourself. Who are you? Why have you come here? How do you know so much about Ansaar ways?"

Laylah glanced down at her tethered hands.

"Telling stories is quite difficult, Majesty, when one is in discomfort. These ropes around me—they bind, they chafe—"

"But you're a prisoner, maula! Prisoners are supposed to be bound!"

"Nevertheless, Sire—if I am to speak at any length of the matters on which you seek to be informed—ah, this pain is hard to bear, and the humiliation, besides!—no, no, I beg you, High One—have my bonds removed from me. And then I'll tell you whatever you wish to know."

The Emperor frowned, and his eyes flickered momentarily with a flash of suspicion. Doubtless he was wondering whether she might be an assassin, who would work some lethal surprise on him the moment her hands were free. Well, a man in his position needed to consider such possibilities, Laylah thought. But she kept her gaze on him steadily in the deferent-but-not-abased mode, and gradually, as he surveyed her with that keen gaze of his own, he seemed to reach the decision that she could be released.

"Cut the ropes from her wrists," he said to a member of his guard.

"And my ankles also, Majesty," said Laylah.

Her impudence seemed only to charm him.

"Of course. The ankles as well," the Emperor said, with a shrug.

The bonds were cut away. Laylah rubbed her hands together, and shifted her weight from foot to foot, savoring the sensation as the blood moved freely in her limbs again.

"Now," the Emperor said. "If you would, my lady—a word or two of explanation from you—"

"In this cold bare room? And without having had anything to eat in almost an entire day?"

His expression showed unmistakable anger now, and Laylah wondered if she had pushed him too far. But then, once again, the Emperor allowed himself to be charmed by the impertinence of the captive maula. "Yes," he said, with a chivalrous flourish. "Certainly, my lady. Better accommodations—some meat and a flask of wine, perhaps?—a warm bath? Would that please you?" He seemed not to be speaking sarcastically. "Very well, then. It will be so. But then you must tell me what you're all about, is that agreed? Why you are here—what you thought you could accomplish by such a journey. I want to know everything. I'll come to you late this afternoon, after I've dealt with the Goishlaar and a couple of those ambassadors, and you'll answer all my questions, with no more of these little requests of yours. Eh, maula? Do you understand?" And once more there was the tone of authority.

The Emperor and the Maula

"I hear and obey, O Lord of Worlds."

"Good. Good." He stared at her strangely for a moment. "How different you are," he said, "from the other humans I have met. Not that there have been many of them, of course. But there have been some. And most of those were in a fury all the time, hostile, uncooperative, unwilling or unable to accept the fact of Ansaar superiority. All they did was shout and rant. How boring they were! And then there was the other kind, the ones who cringed and whined and bowed and scraped, crawling in front of me, agreeing with every word I said. The boot-lickers. They were even worse. But you—you treat me almost as though we were equals! I see neither defiance nor obsequiousness in your manner. You are very unusual, maula. You are extraordinarily unusual."

Laylah said nothing.

The Emperor turned and began to walk away. Then he spun around and said, "By any chance, is there a name by which you are known, maula?"

"Laylah. Laylah Walis."

"And which of those is the soul-name, pray tell, and which the face-name?"

"The face-name is Laylah, Sire. Walis is the soul-name."

"I'll call you Laylah, then. Will that be all right, do you think? May the Lord of the Ansaar Empire call a maula by her face-name?" Again the wry chuckle. The Emperor seemed to be laughing at himself; but Laylah knew, also, that she was in the hands of a lion who amused himself by toying with his prey. As though to underscore the thought, his expression changed once more, suddenly, turning dark and grim, and his eyes flashed with a quick blaze of imperial wrath. "You have to die tomorrow, maula, and there's no way around that. You know that, don't you? Yes, I think you do. That's one of the interesting things about you, that you know it and you don't seem to care. I want to know more about that. Tonight we talk; and tomorrow morning you die. It is the law, and not even the Most Holy Defender of the Race may trifle with the law. Especially not the Most Holy Defender of the Race." He waved his hand at her imperiously. "I will speak again with you later, Laylah Walis." And strode from the room.

▷▷ 5.

THE ACCOMMODATIONS, Laylah had to admit, weren't at all
bad. Were downright palatial, as a matter of fact.

They had put her up, evidently, in one of the suites of
the royal harem. The rumor on Earth—derived, no doubt,
from bawdy tales told by rough Ansaar soldiers of the occupation—was that the Ansaar Emperor had thousands of wives and
concubines; and while that was almost certainly an exaggera-
tion, Laylah suspected it was not exceedingly far from the truth.
They had taken her to her new rooms up a series of winding
marble staircases and down a tangle of bewildering corridors,
and suddenly she found herself being led into a separate wing
of the palace, set apart from the other sectors by high walls
of black brick, where radiating clusters of spoke-like hallways
jutted out in all directions and a maze of brightly lit chambers could be seen in the distance wherever Laylah happened to
look. Women and eunuchs in elegant robes glided about softly

through the halls, dozens of them, scores, not one of them ever meeting Laylah's eye.

"Yours," said the head of the guards who accompanied her, indicating a faintly aromatic door of some dark exotic wood inlaid with strips of ivory.

There were five spacious rooms behind it: a bedroom, a richly curtained sitting room, a bath with an immense crystal tub, a kind of dining chamber arranged around a table cut from a single block of black polished stone, and a tiring-room for the use of her servants, of whom there were three, two maids and a silent, glum-faced figure who wore the neuter-sign on his forehead. They bowed to Laylah as though she were royalty herself, rather than a prisoner under immediate sentence of death who had mysteriously been granted the momentary favor of the Most Holy Defender of the Race.

Without a word, they stripped her and bathed her and anointed her body with oils. They would have anointed her hair, too, but Laylah stopped them in time. She was given robes to wear of some filmy Ansaar fabric that shifted polarity with every movement of her body, so that her nakedness glinted tantalizingly through the material in quick dazzling flashes and then was hidden again. They brought her a platter of some unfamiliar meat and a bowl of odd, angular purple fruits, and a flask of golden wine shot through with startling red highlights, as if powdered rubies had been mixed into it.

Then they left her alone, and the hours slipped by.

She tried the door once. It was locked, of course.

She wandered from room to room, peering in the storage chambers, staring in wonder at the robes and diadems she found in them, a month's wardrobe for a princess royal who never would wear the same thing twice. There was a collection of perfumes and cosmetics—Ansaar perfumes, of course, Ansaar cosmetics, everything vile-smelling and weird, but probably deemed by the Ansaar to be of the highest Ansaar quality. There was a closet full of liqueurs. Laylah wondered whether every member of the royal harem had a suite like this, furnishings like these, accoutrements of this sort. Probably so. Say, three hundred concubines and a hundred wives—

The cost of it all was incalculable. Was it for this that the Ansaar had conquered the galaxy, so that their Emperor could squander a planet's ransom on the women who were his toys?

Fury coursed through her.

But then she grew calm again—what did it matter to her, how the Ansaar chose to waste the profits of their conquests?—and lay down on one of the sumptuous couches and closed her eyes, suddenly overcome by overwhelming fatigue. She had had virtually no sleep since her arrival on Haraar, only a quick fragmentary doze while in the cell at the starport. Now, lulled by wine and her bath, she found herself dropping down and down and down into slumber, much as she tried to fight it.

The Emperor, she thought.

The Emperor will be here any minute—

No matter. She slept, and dreamed of worlds colliding and smashing asunder, and of blazing stars plummeting through the skies, and of fiery comets with the faces of dragons.

Then Laylah heard a faint sound, and opened her eyes, and saw an Ansaar of immense presence and authority standing over her, a formidably tall and astonishingly handsome Ansaar whom her sleep-fogged mind recognized only after a moment or two as His Majesty Ryah VII.

Instantly she was fully awake.

"Majesty!"

"Sit where you are," he said, for she had leaped to her feet at once. "Please. Please. You looked so comfortable, stretched out like that on that divan." He took a seat opposite her. "The rooms are to your liking, I take it?"

"Magnificent, Your Highness."

"Good. You did say that comfort was important to you when telling stories. I asked that you be given one of the best available apartments. This one is usually reserved for one of the junior wives. I thought it would please you."

"Even though I must die tomorrow?" she asked.

He flashed his warmest smile, and then, as before, the smile abruptly turned to a grimace of fury with scarcely any perceptible transition. "It is nothing to joke about, my lady."

"You really do intend to put me to death, then?"

"The law is the law. This planet is not only the seat of the Imperial Government, it's sacred as well. As you surely must know. The lives of those who desecrate it are immediately forfeit." His tone was stern and implacable. "There's muttering aplenty already, I assure you, because I've allowed you to live this long. By this time tomorrow you will be dead. Expect no miracles, lady: I have no choice in this whatever." He leaned toward her and his eyes drilled into her like high-intensity beams. He still seemed angry. "How could you have been so stupid? You're obviously a woman of intelligence and education, as humans go. Of unusual intelligence, it seems to me, as a matter of fact. Why would you want to bring down certain death upon yourself? Tell me that!" the Emperor said savagely. "Tell me!"

"It is, as I said, somewhat of a long story, Majesty."

"Make it no longer than you have to, then." He glanced at a pale green jewel on his wrist. "It is the eighth hour of the night. At the first hour of the morning I must deliver you to the executioner, without fail. Between now and then, Laylah Walis, I want to hear all that you have to tell."

"I will do my best," she said calmly. "Do I have your permission to begin?"

"Yes, of course!"

"Listen, then, O wise and happy Emperor."

And she leaned back on the divan and commenced her tale.

▷▷ 6.

WAS BORN on Earth in a pleasant village in the province of the Green River, which is one of the most fertile provinces of our world, in the year of Earth reckoning 2967 A.D. That is the year Klath 4 of the 82nd Ansaar Imperial Cycle. So I am thirty-four years old by the reckoning of my people, and in Ansaar years I have reached the age of twenty-three. My father was a physician and a shaper of souls, and my mother a scryer, that is, one who studies the fundamental matter of which the universe is composed. At the time of the Ansaar conquest I was a girl just entering womanhood. I had a brother a little younger than myself who intended to be a healer like my father, and an older sister, who was in training for the scrying arts. I myself had not yet chosen a path to follow in my life when the invaders came; but there had always seemed time enough for that later on.

You should understand, O Supreme Omniscience, that Earth at the time of the Ansaar conquest was a world among worlds, a jewel of the stars, a planet to be envied and admired.

Do you know anything of our history? No, of course not, Majesty—how could you? The universe is very wide and our world is small and far away; and the Lord of the Ansaar has much to occupy his mind beside the study of distant and unimportant maula planets. But I assure you, Sire, that Earth was no trivial world, and that its achievements were of the finest. And I need hardly add that to us, our little world was the center of the universe, a place of wonder and beauty and nobility, which we cherished beyond all prizing.

I tell you that, Omniscience, so that you may understand that although to you we are mere barbarians, simple maulas, we had high regards for our world and the level of civilization it had attained. Perhaps there are some races of barbarians who are content to think of themselves as barbarians, but that was not the case with us: we had a history that stretched back across more than ten thousand of our years, and in that time we had surmounted many obstacles, transcended many failings and limitations of our nature, and had built for ourselves a society that seemed to us very near to being perfect. And we were proud of what we had accomplished.

You smile, O Lord of the Galaxy, at our mere ten thousand years! I know, I know, the ten times ten thousand years of Ansaar greatness. But consider this, that when our ten thousand years of greatness had its beginning, we were mere stammering nomads, living on roots and seeds and the beasts of the field; and we rose from that level during those ten thousand years, which are Earth years shorter than yours, to a conquest not only over the forces that rule the sea and the sky and the darkness of space, but to the most difficult conquest of all, a triumph not over other worlds but over our own selves. For we put aside our brutishness and built a great civilization. Has ever a race risen more swiftly from savagery to civilization than ours did?

You should be aware, O Master of the Ansaar, that in our early days we were a warlike and brutal race, much given to acts of bloodshed against one another. In truth we showed no mercy when we fought, and I could tell you terrible tales of unhesitating slaughter, of the burning of villages and the killing of children, of the unending cruelties, the mindless destruction of all that our race had created that was beautiful and splendid. It was like that with us from the very beginning. One of our myths tells of the first people, a mother and a father and their two sons, and how one son lifted his hand against his brother and slew him; and that was in the beginning.

And so it remained through thousands of years. There was no peace among us, not for very long. Again and again the warriors of one family would make war upon another, and the men of one small town marched against those of the next, and country against country when countries came into being out of scattered villages, and then empires would clash with empires in the same way, using ever greater destructive power as our skills and knowledge grew, so that more than once in the history of our world it seemed certain that we would turn all the Earth to rubble and ash.

But that did not happen, O Master of the Ansaar. And that is perhaps our greatest achievement: that our harsh and irascible nature might have led us to destroy ourselves in our uncheckable greed for wealth and power, and we did not do it, although the capability was in our hands. We did not do it.

Nor did the teeming fecundity of our loins fill the world overfull with people, and make our lives squalid and loathsome as a result, as for a time we seemed to be doing, in the unthinking multiplication of our numbers that we permitted. You should know, Lord of All, that by the time of my birth the divisions of the Earth into nations and empires was only a memory, and the populace of the Earth, though great, was no greater than the world could sustain; and that in fact we had made a great green park out of our planet, where the air was fresh and clear and the blue seas were pure and all people lived in harmony and hope.

And then the Ansaar came.

We knew a little, by then, of the existence of the Empire. Not much, for we had chosen not to venture among the stars. Chosen, I say, because it surely would have been in our power to do it, had we wanted to. But we did not want to.

Those earlier Earthfolk, the ones who raised their hands against their brothers and built nations out of towns and empires out of nations, probably looked hungrily toward the stars as well, and said to one another, "Some day we will rule those also!" But by the time the scientific abilities of our race were great enough to allow us to build ships that would travel among the stars, we no longer saw any reason to do it. We were content to remain on our own small world, and to go no farther from it than the other planets that swung in orbit around our little sun.

You are probably thinking, O Omniscience, that that is a profound flaw in us; and perhaps you are right. But we saw it otherwise. For we were happy enough as we were. There were fewer of us than there once had been, and we were not as sorely driven by desires and high ambition. Our days of endless striving were behind us, so we believed, and it satisfied us to live as we were living, in a balanced and harmonious way.

We knew of the Empire in those years because we were able by then to detect some of the messages that pass among the stars, though we could not decipher them; but we understood simply by hearing them that the sky must be full of worlds, and we suspected even that many of those worlds were linked together under the rule of a single dominant race, which later we would learn was the Ansaar. But whatever government might exist among the stars was far away, and had no real significance for us; we wanted no part of the Empire and we believed that the Empire wanted no part of us.

Of course, Majesty, we were wrong about that. For the Empire knows no boundaries, and the questing spirit of the Ansaar knows no peace; and your people will never rest until your power reaches from one wall of the universe to the other.

I remember the day of the conquest—the Annexation, I should say; I know that you prefer us to call it that—as well as I remember any day of my life. It happened in the time of your father of blessed memory, His Departed Majesty Senpat XIV, may he taste the joys of Paradise forever! I was a girl, then—a young woman, really. It was two or three years since my breasts had grown. These are breasts, Majesty, these swellings here: if I were to have a child, they would give milk, for—perhaps you know this?—we humans are mammals. I think you know what mammals are. And the coming of the breasts marks the end of girlhood and the beginning of womanhood, among us.

For me the Annexation began at midday in the brightest time of summer, at a time when my life was tranquil and happy, and the future seemed to unfold before me with almost limitless promise and wonder.

I lived then with my mother and my father and my brother Vann and my sister Theyl—we were a big family; there were not many with so many children—in a house like a golden dome, with a lovely garden of fragrant shrubs all around it, in a quiet village of perhaps a thousand people a short way from the river. To the east of us were low round hills like green humps, and to the west, on the other side of the river, the land tilted upward as though a giant's hand had lifted it, so that mountains of black stone covered with mighty trees rose there to the sky. Once there had been a great city on our side of the river, in the days when the Earth had been crowded and noisy; but the city was long gone, and only its traces remained, a gray line of foundations running through the grass, and a scattering of weathered artifacts that children sometimes discovered while digging in the ground.

It was a peaceful place, a pleasant place, and we hoped that it would never change. But no one in the universe is exempt from change, Great One, not even the mighty Ansaar; and certainly not the people of Earth. Our way of life had changed again and again in the ten thousand years of our history. And now it would undergo its greatest change ever; for, all unknown to us, the Empire had been moving steadily toward us year by year, taking possession of all the worlds that lay in its path, and now at last it was our turn to undergo Annexation.

Do you know what an Annexation is like? But how would you, you who sit here in your wondrous palace at the heart of the Empire, far from the Territories where such things happen? Let me tell you, O great and omnipotent lord, the nature of such an event.

First there is the Darkness. Then there is the Sound. And then, the Splitting of the Sky, and the hosts of the conqueror manifest themselves to the conquered. And at last the Voice, announcing to the conquered ones the fate that has befallen them.

The Darkness is total, both indoors and out—sudden inexplicable night that comes in the middle of the day. Our power sources, of course, were all orbital ones: a string of collector satellites whose great wings gathered the energy of the sun and sent it pulsing toward the surface of Earth in laser-steered bundles. In a single moment the Ansaar invaders simultaneously interrupted the output of every one of our power satellites, all around the world. It is the weapon called the Vax that did that, as I was later to discover. I think you must know of the Vax and what it does, Majesty. The effect for us was as if the satellites in their orbits had all in that one instant been wrapped in blankets of some material wholly impervious to light. Between one moment and the next, every electrical device on our planet ceased to function. Everywhere at once the lights went out on Earth, and everything that was in motion stopped. The Darkness had come to us.

I was in the garden that surrounded my house when that happened, so I had no way of knowing that the lights were out all over the world and that virtually all our machines, including our weapons of defense, had become inoperative. But even out there in the garden, there was Darkness. The sun itself had been blotted out as though by a terrible eclipse. The sky became a pure black sheet: no moon, no stars, so black that it was painful to look at. It felt like a hand across my throat, to stare into such total blackness. Your Vax had thrown some world-encompassing screen of opaque force—some gigantic barrier—across the sky. I have no way of knowing how it achieved that. How could any of us know? It is the great Ansaar weapon, the thing that enables you to rule the galaxy: for you can interpose your might between a planet and its sun, and choke off all light and warmth and energy in a single moment. Who could withstand such a calamity? Day became dense unyielding night at a single stroke, for us.

I stood staring at the suddenly darkened sky, not understanding a thing. I thought at first I had been struck blind. I held my hand up before my face and I could not even see my fingers, not even very faintly, like the shadow of a shadow. There was no light at all anywhere. I closed my eyes and touched my fingers to my eyeballs and I saw colors then, the dancing islands of blue and gold and green that I had always seen when I pressed my eyes; but when I opened my eyes again I could not see a thing. The world in all its brightness and beauty and wonder was gone.

Yet I was not afraid, not yet. For it all had been so sudden, and so total, that my mind could not yet take it in.

Next came the Sound, and the Sound was worse even than the Darkness. It was like nothing that anyone had ever heard before. It started as a low droning wailing warble, coming from a point near the horizon; but gradually it rose enormously in pitch and intensity and in apparent place of origin, until a dreadful ear-splitting screaming was coming down on us from the zenith of the heavens, the siren of our doom, a frightful discordant deafening screeching that would not stop, a noise so powerful that it fell upon us with an almost tangible force.

It went on and on. I thought my head would split apart; and now at last I was thoroughly frightened, not only by the power of the Sound itself, but because this seemed to me to be the end of the world. I fell to my knees and covered my ears with my hands and looked up in terror at the starless midnight sky of this strange summer day, and wondered what was happening. As I think you know already, O Master of All, I am not one who is easily frightened; and yet I was plunged into such an abyss of fear by your Darkness and your Sound that I thought I would never come forth from it, but would shrink down into my own soul like a creature of the soil disappearing into its burrow, and remain there trembling for the rest of my life.

We were conquered already. But of course we had no way of knowing that yet.

I crouched and stared and trembled, as all across the Earth the two billion others of my race were crouching and staring and trembling; for who could do anything else, in the face of such mysteries?

Then, while the Sound continued and, incredibly, grew and grew in strength from moment to moment even when it seemed certain that no sound could possibly be any louder, I saw strange long belts of light appear, rippling across that curtain of total darkness—brilliant horizontal bands of green and yellow and violet and crimson, quivering shimmers of potent brightness that stretched completely across the sky from east to west, extending through my entire field of vision and vanishing beyond the curve of the world's rim. They were like chains encircling the waist of a giant. And, staring at them in wonder and fright, I felt a sense of strain, for I sensed their tense pulsations, as though the giant were breathing in and out, gathering his force, making ready to throw those dazzling shackles off.

And so it was. For now the Splitting of the Sky was starting to occur.

The bands of light danced in and out, the green one bending down upon us until it appeared almost to touch the ground and the adjacent violet one retracting like a drawn bow until it curved far away from us into the heavens, and the crimson and yellow ones doing the same; and then they reversed their positions, snapping inward where they had been out, and out where they were in. All the time the Sound assailed us with ever more horrendous power. This movement of the bands in the sky continued for—five minutes, perhaps? Ten? Or was it only a handful of seconds?—and I became aware, gradually, that the tension of their motion was tearing apart the dense black sheet that lay like a curtain behind them. As those bright bands eddied and rippled to and fro, the blackness was strained and stretched to the sundering point.

And then it ripped, and the stars came shining through. Thousands of them, millions, the heavens ablaze with a myriad white points of gleaming light. The stars, yes, everywhere, cold and dazzling, like the reflections of a million million fires in a dark lake.

The Emperor and the Maula

Or what I thought were stars, in the first moment. I didn't stop to ask myself why the stars would suddenly have become visible in the middle of what had been a bright summer day, so relieved was I to have that bewilderingly opaque black veil torn from the sky. But then I saw that those myriad lights were moving, moving as stars could never move in the sky, that they were rapidly growing larger and larger and must be heading swiftly toward us, as indeed they were: the ships of the invaders, is what those lights were, starships making their descent to Earth. Nor were there really millions of them, or even thousands, but only a few hundreds, the usual size of an Ansaar invasion fleet, multiplied in our dazzled eyes by Ansaar illusion. But of course we did not know that yet either.

The Sound died away, finally. A ghastly stillness took its place, a stillness so total that it was like a roaring in my ears.

And at last came the Voice.

It spoke to us from the sky, a calm clear deep voice that could be heard everywhere on Earth at once. It spoke first for a long while in Universal Imperial, of which, naturally, we could not understand a syllable; and then, after a brief pause, it spoke again in our own language, saying:

"We bring you the warm greetings of His Imperial Majesty Senpat XIV, the High Ansaar, the Supreme Omniscience, the Most Holy Defender of the Race. His Imperial Majesty instructs us to inform the people of Earth that they have been gathered this day into the beneficence of the Empire, and that thenceforth we of the Empire will shield you from all harm, will share with you the greatness of our accomplishments, will guide you toward the attainment of true civilization.

"There is nothing to fear. Your lives and property and safety are not in jeopardy. We want nothing from you but the opportunity to offer you the advantages of the Imperial way of life. A new era begins for you this day, people of Earth: an era of security and happiness and prosperity such as you have never experienced previously, under the benevolent friendship of the Ansaar Empire and His Imperial Majesty, the Lord of All, Senpat XIV, may he thrive and prosper and bring joy to the Ansaar realm forever and a day."

And so we joined your Empire.

We didn't know, in those first moments, that the conquest had already been achieved, that the war of resistance had been lost before it had begun. I assumed—we all assumed—that our leaders must already be recovering from their initial shock, that defensive measures long held in readiness for such an event were already going into action, that everywhere on Earth at this moment the old warlike soul of mankind was awakening from its long slumber and we would within moments begin to take steps to rid ourselves of the unwanted benevolence that the intruders from space were so kindly offering us.

But no—no—

How could we fight back? All our energy sources remained inoperative. Nothing could move on Earth; nothing worked; everything was electrical and everything was dead. Our entire global communications system was silent. There was no longer any government, and certainly no army; there were only the two billion baffled individual citizens of Earth, facing an enemy whose powers were beyond our comprehension, let alone our ability to resist.

The Emperor and the Maula

The shock of what had befallen us landed upon us like a falling mountain. Our souls were numbed by it; our spirits were crushed. That is, of course, the Ansaar way of conquest: to demonstrate in the first moments of the conquest that resistance is unthinkable, and thus to make resistance impossible. And we knew at once that it was so—knew it in our bones and nerves and in the coursing of our blood, as well as in our minds. The habits of conquest and the discipline of ages had made the Ansaar invincible, and it was useless for us to pretend otherwise.

Already the ships of Ansaar were landing in every province of the world, and the Voice of the Imperial Procurator could be heard again everywhere, announcing to us the new order of things.

We were thenceforth under the administration of the Territorial Government of the West Quadrant of the Ansaar Empire. We would pay taxes thenceforth to the Territorial Government, in return for which we would receive the full benefit of membership in the galaxy-wide sphere of mutual prosperity that was the Empire. Once again we were told that there was nothing to fear, that no harm would come to any of us. Those of us who had special skills that might be of use to the Empire would be invited to make those skills available to the Territorial Government; for the rest, life would go on as it always had, except that now an Imperial presence would reside on Earth to insure the perpetual peace and harmony of the planet within the greater entity that was the Ansaar Empire.

The rioting, the panic, began even before the Voice had finished explaining the changes that had come to our world.

We were unable to fight back, that was true. So we showed our unwillingness to accept the benefits of membership in your galaxy-wide sphere of mutual prosperity by allowing the civilization that been ten thousand years in the making to topple into chaos in a single day.

Of course the first thing I tried to do, once the Voice had stopped speaking, was to run for the phone and tell it to call my father at the hospital.

Silence came from the speaker grille. Utter silence, the terrible silence of the darkness between the stars.

"Call my mother, then."

Silence still.

"Get me emergency services!"

Nothing happened; and it was then that I realized that all communications lines must be dead.

I rushed outside. The strange midday darkness still engulfed the world. It seemed to me that it might be thinning—that now I could see shapes through it, although vaguely: as it is said, like the shadows of a shadow. The mountains to the west, the hills to the east, the central service core of the village at the foot of the hills—

Yes. I could see, a little. Not because the sun was shining through the darkness again, but because there was a fire blazing in the village. Tongues of flame licked up into the sky. I heard far-off sounds—shouts, cries—

I had no way of knowing it then, but it was the beginning of the Craziness—the Time of Fire.

The demons that we had put behind us, the monsters and spooks and nightmare beings of our bloody past, all came bursting

The Emperor and the Maula

loose in the moment that we realized our world was no longer our own. Our placid little civilized society—our two billion prosperous people neatly spread out across an entire green planet, our carefully manicured little villages with their tidy homes and pleasing gardens and gentle, law-abiding citizens—went wild with fear, and everything fell apart. The rule of order by which we had lived for hundreds of years collapsed in a moment. Suddenly nothing mattered to anyone except the need to find food, weapons, a secure hiding place. And the hand of neighbor was turned against neighbor, friend against friend, and no one was safe from anyone, and the world became a jungle again in that very hour.

Yes, Majesty, I see your smile, and I can almost read your mind! Maulas, you are thinking. What else could be expected from maulas? Mere primitives, with a pitiful ten-thousand-year veneer of civilization—of course they would turn into savages again the moment things went wrong for them!

Of course!

You are right, and we behaved shamefully, and I will not pretend otherwise. But let me put the question to you, Lord of the Ansaar, and I mean no disrespect, I only ask you to consider this: What if a Darkness were to settle over Haraar a moment and a half from now, and a Sound were to rend your sky, and ships of strange appearance were to appear overhead, and a Voice were to say that the Ansaar Empire had fallen, that your whole domain had now within the space of a few heartbeats become merely a minor province of a far greater empire from another universe, that you had been conquered by a people to whom the mighty Ansaar were no more significant than insects? What would happen, O

Emperor of All, if that should occur? The myriad obedient slaves in your palace—the eunuchs, the concubines, all the lesser and greater wives—would they gather around you and protect you, O Supreme Omniscience? Or would they not fall upon you in the first moment of the Annexation and tear you into a thousand pieces, and then run through the palace like wild beasts, shouting and screaming, tearing down the fine draperies, and prying the jewels free from the walls, and slaughtering anyone who tried to prevent them?

I mean no disrespect, O Emperor of All.

I merely raise the point, for the sake of asking you to think of what it would be like if it were the Ansaar who were conquered in a moment after ninety thousand years of supremacy. If a race greater even than yours were to come without warning, and to seize your world with no more expenditure of effort than a smile and a wink, and to kick your Empire to pieces the way a boy kicks an insect-nest apart—casually, indifferently?

But I am not here to ask you questions, Sire. I am here to tell you my story; and so I will.

How I managed to live through the first twenty days after the Annexation—the days that we called the Craziness then, and which now are called on Earth the Time of Fire—I can hardly say. There was madness everywhere, and thousands died in those early days, maybe hundreds of thousands. Some, I know, died honorably in fighting against the invaders; but for each one of those, there must have been twenty, or fifty, who met their deaths at the hands of fellow humans, for in the Time of Fire it was a war of everyone against everyone.

The Emperor and the Maula

There was no longer any rule of law, except the law that the Ansaar imposed, and in the early days we saw very little of the Ansaar. They had taken command of the centers of our civilization, and from time to time their Voice spoke to us, but they themselves were all but invisible to us. I never saw one myself until the third month of the occupation.

Attempts were made by our government officials to communicate with us by scattering leaflets from the sky that urged us to join in a resistance movement; but they failed; and very quickly we came to understand that we had no government left at all. But that much was clear to me as soon as I saw the fires rising and burning unchecked where our village had been. At least I was in the safety of my home, at the village's edge, close by the river. I locked the doors and windows and waited, without power and with only a little food, hardly daring to sleep, for my parents or my brother or sister to come home.

They never did; and indeed I never saw my mother and father again, or my sister. My father, I learned long afterward, had died in the early hours of the Annexation when a terrified mob had broken into his hospital in search of medical supplies. My mother, whose researches were of interest to the occupying authorities, was "annexed" herself by the Ansaar, and taken to one of the new depositories where humans with scientific or technical skills were being collected.

As for my brother and my sister—

My brother Vann, because he pretended to the Ansaar that he was already a trained healer, was taken to the same center as my mother. But he was there only a short while, and then was transferred somewhere else. To another world of the Empire, as a matter of fact. It would be years before I found him again, and then—but that is another story, Sire, and a very painful one.

It was even harder for me to learn anything about the fate of Theyl, my sister. Since she was learning to be a scryer, she was, I suppose, annexed and taken to one of the depositories also; but there was no record later that that had been done, so perhaps she was one of those killed during the Time of Fire. But I like to think that she is alive, somewhere in this vast Empire. And perhaps some day I will see her again.

As for me, I survived. Somehow.

When the food ran out at home, I went out of the house for the first time since the coming of the Ansaar, and found berries and seeds to eat, like any savage. I crept down to the river and filled pots and jars with water, and took them back to the house. If I had seen any small wild animals, I would have thrown rocks at them and tried to kill them; but wild animals have not been common on Earth for a thousand years.

The Darkness was over, now. It had done its job; and the Ansaar once again were allowing the sun to shine by day and the moon and stars to be seen at night. In those early days I would have preferred the Darkness, I think. I would have felt safer, moving about under cover of that total blackness. Whenever I was outside of the house and caught a glimpse of one of my neighbors, I would run desperately and hide in the bushes, like some wild animal myself in fear for its life, and crouch there until I thought it was safe for me to come out.

But gradually the Craziness ebbed, and we became accustomed to our new lives under the Ansaar. We began to trust each other again; we began to come together like the civilized beings we once had been, and which we hoped to be once more.

"The cities have all been destroyed, and their people evacuated into the countryside," I learned from Harron Devoll, the woman who lived just across the stream from my house. "And all the government officials have been killed. They lined them up against a wall and shot them." A great weight of loss and sadness descended on me when I heard that. But was it true? Who could say? I asked Harron who had told her, and whether they were reliable, and she replied simply, "Everybody knows that it's so."

There were other stories, too. That you Ansaar were emptying Earth's museums and carrying off shiploads of art treasures to their own main planet; that you were doing something to the oceans and rivers with chemicals to make Earth's water more agreeable to you; that we would all be taken away into slavery, to work as laborers in Ansaar mines on distant worlds; that Ansaar soldiers were raping Earth women, whom they found extraordinarily desirable.

Was any of it true? Who could say?

All I knew was that the world I had known had come to an end, and that I was living in some new world now where anything might happen and none of it would be good.

But life went on, somehow, all the same. The killing of neighbor by neighbor ended, and in our village we joined in little groups to raise crops, and to share such packaged foods as yet remained to us, and to make plans, as best we could, for the unknown and terrifying future. We rebuilt much of the village center where it had been burned by the rioters on the first day of the Annexation. But some things could not be rebuilt. Electrical service still had not been restored, nor were the communications nets open. The hospitals were in ruins. Everything that mattered had been destroyed. We had been plunged back into a harsh medieval way of life in a single moment.

Of the Ansaar themselves we still saw nothing, in our little village.

Finally they arrived, as I have said, in the third month of the Annexation. Three of them came to us in a small bronze-colored teardrop-shaped vehicle that floated a little way off the ground. They halted it in the center of the village and stepped out and made a little tour of inspection, peering at our town hall, at the broken windows of our empty shops, at us.

Oh, they were strange to behold! And even so, it was surprising, how ordinary they were. We had expected demigods; and then the conquerors of Earth came to us, and they were just ugly little creatures with crested heads and jutting big-muzzled faces like an animal's, and thick necks and short legs, and long arms that dangled almost to the ground!

Forgive me, Greatness. But do you understand that we expected more of them than that? They had seized our world in a moment: and surely beings who could do that had to be of titanic stature and grandeur. We wanted them to be tall and beautiful and splendid, with shining eyes and heroic frames. And instead they were squat, they were coarse, they were ugly. They moved not with the grand swagger of overlords but rather in the unassuming slouching way of those who were merely doing a routine job, ordinary troops patrolling an ordinary little conquered planet. It is bad enough to be conquered, we told ourselves. But to have been conquered by mediocre creatures like those—

I see you smiling again, Excellency. I know what you are thinking. Such airs this maula puts on, you tell yourself. She dares to complain that the soldiers of the Ansaar were not grand and awesome enough for her taste! But I want to speak only the truth to you, and that is how we felt.

"We could kill them," someone among us said. "There are only three of them, and there are so many of us. If we killed them all, a few at a time—"

"Perhaps we really could kill them, yes," someone else answered. "And then the others will come, and they will burn the village down to the ground, and burn us with it." And we knew that that was true; and so we did nothing.

The three Ansaar set up headquarters for themselves in our town hall, and had us come to them one by one to give our names and answer some questions about ourselves. When it was my turn, I could not stop staring, for they seemed so strange to me, and so repellent. Yes, Majesty, repellent. But I had no reason to love them, did I? They were our conquerors, our overlords. And yet, though I was appalled by them, I felt a great curiosity about them too, wondering, Who are these people, these Ansaar, who have crossed half the sky to take our world away from us, and why did they want to do it, and how have they become so mighty that no race can resist their power? They had a machine which turned what I said into words they could understand, and what they said into good clear Earth-words, and we talked for a time. They said to me, "What special skill do you have, Laylah Walis?"

And I said, without even stopping to think, "I know how to learn. That is my skill."

And as I said it, I swore to myself that I would discover for myself all that could be known about the race that had come from the stars to make themselves our masters.

I did not expect, though, to be given a chance so quickly, and at such close range, to begin gaining knowledge of what the Ansaar are like.

It happened three days after the arrival of the Ansaar in our village. I was in my house; and there came a heavy knock at the door, a pounding that shook the building. I asked who it was, and heard an Ansaar voice ordering me to open up.

I was frightened, of course. I was alone and the thought of having the Ansaar enter my house filled me with dread. I remembered what Harron Devoll had told me about the Ansaar finding the women of Earth physically desirable—I imagined what horror it would be to be raped by an Ansaar—

But I was more afraid of not opening the door than I was of opening it; for if I refused, the Ansaar might destroy my house and me within it. So I turned the handle and let the Ansaar in. I realized at once that he was one of the three who had interviewed me at the town hall. It was by a great welt of a purple birthmark across his upper face, like a cap worn low on his forehead, that I recognized him. He was very short and very wide through the shoulders, and his skin had a greenish cast and a pebbled texture.

For a moment we stood face to face, the Ansaar and I. Can you understand the horror I felt, Majesty? A defenseless girl, staring into those alien yellow eyes, seeing that jutting muzzle, imagining those leathery, sharp-clawed seven-fingered hands touching my naked flesh?

And then the Ansaar made a low rumbling sound deep in its throat, and took a step toward me, arms outstretched and claws spread wide, and another step, and another—

$\triangleright\!\!\triangleright$ 7.

A BRUPTLY LAYLAH broke off her tale.

"I think that morning is here, Sire."

It was purely a guess. But the Emperor glanced at the jewel on his wrist and said, "So it is." He frowned, then, and in a barely audible tone added, "And so our conversations must end. For at the first hour of the morning you have an appointment with the executioner."

She regarded him unwaveringly.

"I have not forgotten that either," she said. "Well, then—I hope that I have entertained you at least a little this night, O Lord of All. And if it is not beneath the dignity of an Emperor of the Ansaar to pray for the repose of a maula's soul, I hope you will have a good word for me in your prayers this day, Majesty, as I go to my death."

The Emperor looked irritated and perplexed. Then he said, after a moment of fidgety hesitation, "But you surely aren't going to break off your story now, are you? At least will you finish what you were just telling me, before I go? I want to know what happened between you and the Ansaar soldier!"

"But the first hour is here already, Majesty," said Laylah sweetly. "And my time has come."

She had declined to obey a direct Imperial order. Plainly he wasn't accustomed to that.

But he seemed willing to let the point pass.

"For an Ansaar soldier to assault a woman of an Annexed species is completely unlawful," he said, "and outrageous besides. If any criminal actions occurred, the man will be identified and severely punished even at this late date, I promise you that. And so I want to find out exactly what took place between the two of you. Your execution—" he seemed to have trouble with the word—"can wait until you tell me."

"Oh, but it is a very long story, Majesty!"

Again the mixture of amusement and annoyance showed in his expression.

"All your stories are very long stories, is that not so? How long can it take? Leave out all those circumstantial details that you paint so well, and simply give me the essence. Did he rape you, yes or no?"

"Majesty—forgive me—I need to have the time to place the event in its proper context—"

The Emperor scowled. In growing exasperation he said, "How much time? An hour? Two? There is no time, woman! The Debin of Hestagar is due to arrive at the court at the third hour of the morning to discuss the assessment of tribute for the coming year, and I need half an hour or so to review the Hestegar situation before I see him, and before that I have the morning observances to perform, and then—"

"I could finish the story tonight, then," Laylah suggested.

His eyes grew stern and bleak, that imperious glare that she had seen before.

"For you, lady, as you know only too well, there will be no tonight."

"Ah. How true," she said.

And she fell silent.

"Well—" the Emperor said thoughtfully, after a little while. "Well, then—"

▷▷ 8 .

T WAS a long day for Laylah. The Emperor, when he had left her, had promised to return in the evening to hear the outcome of her story; but he clearly seemed troubled by the bending of the law that granting so temporary a reprieve as this involved. Even the Most Holy Defender of the Race, it appeared, was not free to violate tiihad with impunity—perhaps precisely because he was, among other things, the Most Holy Defender of the Race. He had said it himself, the day before: Tonight we talk; and tomorrow morning you die. It is the law, and not even the Most Holy Defender of the Race may trifle with the law. Especially not the Most Holy Defender of the Race.

At any rate, dawn had come and gone and she was still alive. That was a promising start.

But it was obvious from the puzzled expressions of her maids that morning and from the long face of her scowling neuter chamberlain that they were surprised to find her still in residence past the hour of execution, and none too pleased about it, either. Laylah's studies of Ansaar culture had already indicated to her that it was the lower castes, as usual, who took tiihad with the greatest seriousness. Aristocrats might shrug at the social codes, so long as their own positions remained secure, but the common folk, fearing a wholesale collapse of the social order that might bring chaos into their own lives, generally preferred that everybody observe the rules of behavior—even where that might be disadvantageous to themselves.

Her own servants, then, wanted her to die, for the sake of blotting out the dire impiety of her presence on the holy world. What about the higher officials of the court? What pressures was the Emperor Ryah under at this very moment from his viziers and councillors, now that they were coming to realize that the maula had not in fact been put to death on schedule?

And would the Emperor yield to them, finally? How powerful was his curiosity about her story, anyway? Perhaps her blatantly disingenuous tactics of delay would come to infuriate rather than tantalize him, when he had been away from her for an hour or two, and had a chance to think things over. Would the minions of the executioner turn up at the door of her suite after all, some time later in the day?

She dozed a little after the Emperor had taken his leave, but—although she had scarcely slept at all since her arrival on Haraar—it was almost impossible now to get any rest. Any time she heard the clicking footsteps of someone passing by in the corridor outside, the sound translated itself, to her half-conscious mind, into the knock of the emissaries of death at her door. And once, when she did fall into something more or less like a sound sleep, she dreamed that the knock did come, and she went to the door and opened it, and there, grinning at her in keen anticipation, was a gigantic Ansaar with shoulders like a bull's, holding in his powerful hands a gleaming hatchet dripping red with blood.

So Laylah abandoned the idea of further sleep. She allowed herself to be bathed and anointed with aromatic oils, and she had herself dressed in a simple but fine robe; and then she waited for the hours to pass. Leaving her rooms, of course, was impossible. It was a gilded cage that she was living in, no doubt of that; but it was a cage all the same.

The day went by, somehow.

And then Laylah's sour-faced chamberlain appeared, and announced in his grandest tones, "His Majesty the Emperor calls upon you once again!"

"Bring me wine," the Emperor said brusquely, as he came striding through the ivory-inlaid door of her suite. "Be quick about it!" And clapped his hands.

The maids scurried to obey.

"A difficult day, Majesty?" Laylah asked, for all the world like a queen welcoming her royal husband home from the grand audience-chamber.

He glanced at her, startled. Then he smiled faintly, perhaps amused by the intimacy of her tone.

"The Debin," he muttered, in a bitter tone. "The Goishlaar of Gozishtandar. The Great Frulzak of Frist! The High Muerthiopoz! The Gremb! All day long, princes and princelings and potentates of the tributary worlds—dozens of them, processions of them, prostrating themselves, abasing themselves, murmuring hypocritical words of obscenely overstated praise, shoving heaps of gifts toward the throne, and all of them wanting something from me, wanting, wanting, wanting—" The Emperor shook his head and took a moody gulp of his wine. "I was third in line for the throne, do you know that? I never expected to inherit. It should have been Senpat, you know. He had the royal name—there were Senpats on the throne for nine generations in a row—and he had the training, too. But Senpat loved racing his little hyper-yacht too much, and taking too many chances with it; and one day he came out of hyper right in the middle of the sun, the poor fool. Well, there was my brother Iason, the second prince; but the moment he heard that Senpat was dead, he enrolled in a stasis monastery, and there he sits to this day, sealed in beyond all reach for the next ten thousand years, neither dead nor alive but as holy as anyone can possibly be. So my father summoned me to the throne-chamber—why am I telling you this, I wonder?—he summoned me, and there were red tears rolling down his cheeks, and he said, 'Ryah, my youngest—Ryah, my dearest—' I thought the tears were for Senpat and for Iason, but I soon saw that they were for me. He begged me not to fail him in this time of need. Nor did I; and here I am. The wives! The concubines! The grand palaces! The absolute power over a trillion lives! But also—the Debin—the Goishlaar! The Great Frulzak of Frist! The High Muerthiopoz! The Gremb!"

"Kings are like stars," said Laylah. "They rise and set, they have the worship of the world, but no repose."

The Emperor looked up from his cup of wine, eyes wide with astonishment.

"Well said! Well said! You have the true gift of words, Laylah."

"Oh," she said, smiling. "They are very fine words, yes, but not my own. I simply quote one of our ancient poets, a man named Shelley."

"Ah. Ah. He understood a great deal, your Shelley. Did you have many poets as good as he?"

"A great many, yes." And the words of some of those other poets came to her mind, and she thought, but did not say,

Titles are shadows; crowns are empty things;
The good of subjects is the end of kings.

And she also thought, and also did not recite,

Let us sit upon the ground
And tell sad stories of the death of kings:
How some have been depos'd, some slain in war,
Some haunted by the ghosts they have depos'd.
Some poisoned by their wives, some sleeping kill'd,
All murdr'd.

"So many worlds—so many poets," said the Emperor. "I wish I could study them all. You must recite some of your other great poets' work too, Laylah, when there is time."

"But there is no time, Sire. First I must finish my story; and then—and then—"

"Your story, yes," the Emperor darkly. "And then—then—" He peered into his wine-cup as though it held the answer to all the mysteries, and swirled it around, and said, after a time, "All day long, between the ambassadors and the potentates and the petitioners, what did I hear from my own people? The maula, they said. The maula, the maula, the maula! Where is she? What has been done with her? Why has there been no execution yet?" He glared at her, a strange tortured look, fury mixed with compassion. "Oh, Laylah, Laylah, Laylah, why did you ever come here? And why did I not have your head cut from your body the moment I learned that you had set foot on Haraar?"

"My story, Lord of All—may I resume my story?"

He waved his hand in a fretful, abstracted way.

"Your story," he said again. "Yes. Your story. By all means. Finish telling me your story. And see that you finish it, this time!"

▷▷ 9.

WELL, THEN, O great and glorious Emperor, let us go back to my house in the village near the river, not long after the Annexation. When I was alone, and heard the knock on the door, and admitted the Ansaar soldier. There I stood like one who is frozen, and the Ansaar soldier was coming toward me, reaching his arms toward me and spreading wide his claws, and I was certain that in another moment he would seize me and hurl me to the floor and throw himself on top of me and do loathsome bestial things to me. But I was unable to move.

How could I have known, unfamiliar as I was then with Ansaar ways then, that his gesture of outstretched arms and wide-spread claws, menacing though it seemed, was merely a normal Ansaar mode of demanding attention from a stranger—that the thought of assaulting me, or any human woman, for that matter, was nowhere in his mind?

He halted when he was still a short distance from me.

"You are Laylah Walis?" he asked, speaking with difficulty in heavily accented English. He did not have his translating machine with him. "It is your name—Laylah Walis?"

"Yes."

He was, he told me, Procurator-Adjutant Jjai Haunt of the Ansaar Expeditionary Force, and he had come here to annex me into the service of the Empire.

His words flowed from him in such a thick-tongued way that I barely understood them. But I understood enough.

"Annexed?" I gasped. "Me? Why?"

"You will be trained for interfacing duties," said Haunt, visibly struggling to make himself comprehensible. He consulted some scrap of paper that he had been carrying tucked in a belt at his waist. "At your placement interview," he said, "you claimed the ability to learn as your special gift. Therefore you will be useful. We need those who can learn; and we will teach you. And then you will help us in our task of administering the Territory of Earth."

They would train me to be a traitor to my people, in other words.

But I was too naive to realize that, then. Or perhaps I was simply so relieved that I was not going to be the victim of some violent assault that I gave no thought at that moment to the real meaning of Haunt's words.

Not that my consent was required in any case, of course. I had been annexed, and that was that. Haunt ordered me to gather my things—I had five minutes to select whatever I wanted to take with me—and then he led me outside into his little teardrop-shaped floater-car.

The Emperor and the Maula

I never saw my house again, or my village, or anyone I had ever known in the sixteen years I had lived thus far.

There was an Ansaar annexation depository on the other side of the mountains, about half an hour's floater-drive away, and that was where Haunt took me. "I will see you again, Laylah Walis," he told me solemnly, when he dropped me off. As though that would matter to me.

The annexation depository was a sort of giant barracks, a long string of crude windowless rooms constructed of some gray foam-like material that had obviously been squirted into place by Ansaar construction robots in a mere hour or two. At least five hundred humans from a number of different villages were being housed there, maybe more, under the control of no more than about a dozen Ansaar who did not even bother to carry weapons. But there was hardly any risk of an uprising by the annexed. No one had the heart for such a thing. Everybody I saw had the same dull, dazed, stunned expression in their eyes, as though they had been drugged.

No drugs had been given them, though. It was the conquest itself that had stunned and dazed them like a blow across the forehead—the suddenness of Earth's loss of its ancient independence, which had left them all bewildered, unable to comprehend what had befallen them. It was like living among ghosts, Excellency, to live with these annexed people.

I asked some of them whether they knew if my mother or my brother or my sister might be in the camp. No one could tell me anything useful. One man thought that he might have encountered my mother in his first days at the depository—her name, at least, seemed to strike a chord in his memory—but he was vague and uncertain about it. And in any event she was no longer there now, if she ever had been. She had been moved along, I suppose, to whatever task our Ansaar masters had had in mind for her.

Three days of emptiness passed. I walked endlessly around the perimeter of the depository—a kind of foggy gray aura marked its boundary, and I had already been warned not to try to pass through it—and stared at the dark wall of the mountains and counted clouds and tried once more to come to terms with the thing that had happened to our world. And then on the fourth day Haunt came back for me, as he had promised.

His distinct birthmark was covered by a loosely wrapped headcloth, and so I didn't recognize him. At that time all Ansaar soldiers looked pretty much the same to me.

He seemed to expect that, though. He said right away, "I am Haunt. Who was with you before. You will come with me, Laylah Walis. Your instruction will now begin."

I realized that Procurator-Adjutant Haunt was going to be my teacher himself.

He took me to a little three-cornered building on the other side of the camp from the sleeping-quarters. This would be our classroom. "First our language," he said, indicating a copper helmet that he wanted me to put on.

It must have been specially designed for humans, because it fit tightly over the top of my head, where no Ansaar could have worn it on account of the Ansaar crest. I slipped it on and without warning I was hit by a burst of energy so powerful that I thought I was going to die.

The Emperor and the Maula

The world went black, and I felt a sensation like icy daggers plunging into both my eardrums at once, and there was a wild swirling around me, as though I were caught in some frightful snowstorm; but this was more like a storm of ashes, dark and thick and rough and stifling. Choking and gasping, I put my hands to my head to pull the helmet away, but removing it was impossible—it stuck to me like my own skin.

Haunt removed it for me, a moment or two later. It seemed as though I had had it on me for hours; but it had been hardly any time at all.

"Now we can begin to teach you our words," he said, still speaking his clumsy English.

By this time I had come to expect miracles from the Ansaar; and so I thought that the helmet had filled my mind with your language in a single jolt. But no, no, it was nothing like that, Majesty. I still could not understand a word of Universal Imperial. What the helmet had given me was the capacity to learn the language of the Empire. For your language is so different in all its basic structural assumptions, O Lord of All, that our minds must be re-adjusted in order to grasp its underlying principles. Such Ansaar linguistic concepts as the unifying divider—the distributive affiliate—the shifter and the reduplicative and the somatic grammatical phase—they are so alien to the way we humans think and speak that we could never grasp them without mechanical help.

Yet—as you see, O Master of the Universe, I speak your language fluently now, thanks to the copper helmet and to Procurator-Adjutant Haunt's patient and effective instruction.

When I could speak Universal well enough to converse with him in a reasonably intelligent way, he taught me also some of the history of the Empire: its origins on holy Haraar, its unchecked spread from world to world of your system and then to the surrounding stars, its ninety thousand years of constant expansion throughout the galaxy. He explained the guiding philosophy of the Principate, the powerful need of your people to introduce order and simplicity into the turbulence and confusion of a universe that is filled with so many kinds of intelligent species; and he pointed out to me some of the great advantages that have come to the annexed races as a result of their affiliation with the Empire.

Even after he had told me these things, Majesty, I still lamented the loss of our world's independence. But at least I began to comprehend how valuable the Empire has been in warding off chaos in the universe, by preventing the war of world against world and by ensuring the free flow of commerce throughout the almost infinite bounds of the Empire.

And then Haunt took me aloft, in a little gravity-thrust vehicle that carried us far up into the darkness that surrounded the Earth, and and we traveled around the circumference of the Earth, looking down together on the newest of the worlds of the Ansaar Empire.

I had never been above the surface before. I stared in wonder and awe at the broad blue-green bosom of the Earth, looking down at shining fields of white snow, and vast tawny wastelands, and at forests that were such a deep green that they appeared to be black, and the great dark expanses of the oceans, which hurled blinding sun-blinks back up at us.

The Emperor and the Maula

The ship in which we rode had screens that could be adjusted to magnify our view of what lay below us, so that when we looked through them it seemed we were skimming through the air at a height hardly greater than that of the treetops. There was nothing that we could not see through those screens: villages and even streets and individual people, and heads of grain nodding in the fields, and even finer details.

And also we saw, limned like faint ghost-sketches against the distant ground, the outlines of ancient cities, the dim vestiges and shadowy ruins of the crowded, noisy, brawling Earth of the vanished past.

"Tell me what those cities were called," Haunt ordered me. "I am instructed to compile an account of this planet's history, going back, perhaps, the past fifty thousand years. We already have some information, of a fragmentary sort, about the time when Earth was covered with large cities. Tell me: Which was London? Which was Rome? Which was New York? We know the names, but not the locations."

Of course I had lived my entire life in a single small village, rarely venturing even across the river, let alone to far-off places, and I had little more idea of where New York or London or Rome might have been than Haunt did. They were only names to me, schoolbook names out of a remote and almost meaningless past. We had put all that behind us, on Earth: those cities were symbols to us of the troubled and anguished era of conflict and irrational hatreds out of which we had evolved to the tranquility and joy that had been ours until the Ansaar came. And, looking down from our immense heights, seeing only the shadowy gray outlines of places that had been abandoned for five hundred years or more, the stumps of once-majestic buildings, the sketchy hints of what must have been highways and bridges, great amphitheatres and monuments, I could tell him very little, at least on that first flight.

But he needed to know. And so I found books in our archives and studied them, and day by day I taught myself about the old busy Earth that had been, so that I could teach these things to Procurator-Adjutant Jjai Haunt of the Ansaar Expeditionary Force.

"That one, with the river running through it, that was London, where the English people lived. And over there—it had a river too—that was Paris, in a country that was called France. Do you see, the spidery metal tower? And the gray building on the island—the cathedral is what that was. Where they had the religious ceremonies." We swung down into the middle of the world and I showed him Egypt's Pyramids, rising starkly out of the sands in stony disdain, no more troubled by this latest conqueror than they had been by any of the others of the past six thousand years; and I found China's Great Wall for him, endlessly zigzagging its way across the deserts of Asia; and I took him afterward to the sites where New York, Chicago, Los Angeles, and a dozen other cities of the Western Hemisphere, had been, telling him with breathless pride how many millions of people had lived in each in the bygone days when we Earthfolk had liked to come together in great cities: eight million here, I said, and nine million there, and this one, down there, fifteen million, and twenty million in that one in the broad valley beneath those two lofty mountains.

Haunt seemed impressed. He was thoughtful and silent much of the time, making occasional notes, rarely commenting aloud on what I was telling him. I wanted him desperately to look up once, just once, and say to me, "I see now that this was no piddling little world, this Earth of yours!"

But he never said any such thing. I was only a naive child then; and how was I to know that this was Procurator-Adjutant Jjai Haunt's twentieth planetary assignment, and that he had taken part already in the conquests of at least a dozen huge glittering worlds whose attainments and achievements made those of Earth seem like the doings of children? Well, Haunt had the goodness not to humble my pride by telling me any of that. I learned it for myself, later on, when I began my travels through the Empire, and saw what real planetary magnificence was like. But that was later. For now, I was content to be discovering the wonders and splendors of Earth's own glorious past.

Once, on one of our trips into the sky, Haunt took me right to the edge of our little ship's range to show me the device by which the Ansaar maintained their power over the worlds that they have annexed. We were deep in the darkness above the Earth when he indicated a shining globe floating in orbit not far from our small vessel. It seemed to be no bigger than my fist. I could have reached out with a broom and gathered it in.

"That is the Vax," said Haunt. "It is through the Vax that we rule your world."

"What does it do?"

"It disrupts all electrical fields not of our own making," Haunt told me. "It severs all communications links. If necessary, it propagates a beam in all directions at once at a wavelength that overrides the visual spectrum, creating the darkness that covered the Earth at the time of our landing."

It was so tiny! But I could see the white whorls of Vax-power radiating from it, spinning off like writhing knots through the blackness of the sky, dropping down onto our world and controlling it. And it seemed to me that I could hear the Vax singing with its own immense power, a slow, heavy, infinitely leisurely song of domination that rode on the bow-wave of those white whorls.

"Surely your letting me see this is a breach of security, Haunt," I said to him. "We could steal one of these little gravity-ships, and ride up here and knock your Vax from the sky, and then what would become of your invasion? For there are so many of us and so few of you, and if you were unable to make things dark for us again—"

Haunt looked amused.

"No. Behind this Vax there is another, and behind that one a third. They are in—adjacent spaces, well beyond your reach. We always install backups in whatever we do. You could never locate them; nor could you harm them if you did."

I knew that he was telling the truth; and I knew that Haunt had taken me here to show me how futile any kind of treachery would be, that the Ansaar dominion on Earth was unshakeable and that I had no choice but to serve and obey. But he had demonstrated this to me in a kindly and subtle way.

Indeed I came to like Procurator-Adjutant Haunt very much. I would not have thought that that was possible, for a girl of Earth to develop warm feelings for one of the invaders. And perhaps it

The Emperor and the Maula

is an overstatement, Majesty, to say that I liked Haunt, that my feelings for him were warm; but in a certain way he did come to seem like a friend to me, as much as any Ansaar could have been. I felt no hatred in my heart for him, though I did not cease to regret and deplore the Annexation itself.

He taught me a great deal; and throughout my life I have always respected and admired my teachers.

Haunt was my protector, too. I came to depend on him for that.

Let me explain, Sire. I have said several times that I was naive, then, and one mark of my naivete was that I allowed myself to be turned into a traitor to my people without any awareness of what I was becoming.

You look troubled, Omniscience, as you seemed to be before, the other time when I used that word.

I know it is difficult for you to see service to the Empire as any kind of treason. But bear in mind that I am not an Ansaar, but a member of an annexed race; and that we of Earth are particularly proud and stubborn, in our way, and though we had no choice but to accept Annexation, we always resented it. It is not in our nature to be reconciled easily to conquest. Yet there I was, serving our conquerors.

I was, in truth, making myself highly useful to them. Without cooperators such as myself they would have had little access to any of the data that could help them understand this latest of their conquests. For our language is as alien to the Ansaar as the Ansaar tongue is to us, and as language goes, so goes conceptualization itself. Much that was readily comprehensible to us was baffling even to a fine Ansaar mind; and so it was necessary from the start for the Ansaar to turn to guides, interfaces, who could explain human ways to their conquerors.

Though I was young and inexperienced even in the ways of my own world, I was, as I truthfully told my interviewers, skilled at learning things; I learned quickly and the clarity of my mind is such that I am good at explaining to others such things as I have learned. So members of the Ansaar high command would come to me with questions about the planet they now ruled, and I would answer them, and if I did not know the answers, I would find them.

It took me a great deal of time to realize that this was treason in the eyes of many of my fellow citizens.

I was no longer living in the annexation depository now. I had been taken to New Haraar, the administrative capital that the Ansaar had constructed in one of the southern provinces, and here I worked daily at my task of finding answers to whatever questions the Ansaar cared to ask me. Haunt remained my liaison with the overlords of Earth. I met with him every day and we went over the problems of the current project together; I rarely saw anyone else, Ansaar or human.

Plenty of humans were there, of course. They had been brought in from all over the world to serve the Ansaar. None of them came from any village I had ever heard of, nor had they heard of mine, and though I have never been a shy or antisocial person, I had difficulty making friends with any of them. I thought at first that this was because I came from a village that they did not know. I didn't realize, not for a long while, that they were deliberately avoiding me.

The Emperor and the Maula

I was cooperating willingly with our overlords, you see. And my relations with an officer of the occupying force were openly friendly. Whereas most humans at the capital simply looked upon themselves as prisoners of war, who served the Ansaar grudgingly and with hatred in their hearts.

But I found out the truth one day about six months after I had come there, when I was walking down the street between my lodging and the main Ansaar data repository. I was supposed to meet Haunt there and report to him on some research I had done concerning the different racial forms of the human species and the problems that those differences had caused in ancient times. And suddenly a group of people—five, eight, ten, I never knew how many—came rushing out of an opening between two buildings and began shouting and shaking their fists at me.

"Ansaar whore!" they cried. "Alien-lover! Traitor!"

They were all around me, pushing and screaming. Someone spat in my face. Someone pulled my hair. I thought they were going to kill me.

"Ansaar whore!" they kept yelling. "Whore! Whore! Where's your Ansaar lover, whore?"

I had never fought with anyone in my life; but I fought now, as best I could, trying to keep them away from me as they punched me and slapped me and tossed me around. "Wait—" I called to them. "Why are you doing this? What's wrong?" But they only laughed and hit me harder. My lips was split now and blood was running down my cheek. One of my eyes felt puffed and swollen. I was turning round and round, and wherever I turned someone hit me.

And then Haunt was there.

To my immense relief he came out of nowhere into the middle of the whirlwind, just as the crowd's anger was rising to an even higher pitch of frenzy and I was beginning to see that I was in real danger. For a moment I think none of them realized that he was there. He was a short man even as Ansaar of his caste go, not a very conspicuous figure at all. But his hands came up high and his claws flashed brightly in the sun and he caught hold of one of my attackers and touched him, very lightly, along the side of his face, and the man dropped to the ground. Haunt touched another, and he fell too. And another.

By now they knew what was happening. They stepped back, looking surly, glaring at Haunt and me with such loathing that it made me tremble.

"You must not harm her," Haunt said simply, in English. "Is that clear? She is not to be hurt. Your names have been recorded and if she is harmed, you will suffer. Now go. Go."

They went. Fast.

"Are you all right?" he asked me.

"Frightened," I said. "Shaken up. Some cuts and bruises. Nothing very serious, I suppose." I could almost have hugged him, so great was my gratitude. Almost. "Oh, Haunt, Haunt—were they insane? Why did they jump on me like that?"

"They dislike our—friendship," he said. "We are friends, you and I, are we not?"

"Of course."

"They are not pleased by that."

No, they were not pleased. All that day I could hear their angry shouts in my mind.

Traitor! Ansaar whore! Where's your Ansaar lover, whore?

Did they think that Haunt and I were—

Yes. They did. No one troubled me for a few days; and then, as I was having lunch in the cafeteria where everyone in my department ate, a woman I didn't know sat down next to me and said in a low voice, "Are you really sleeping with him, girl?"

"What?"

"The Ansaar. The one who debriefs you. Do you and he do it or don't you?"

I was astounded. "You mean, are we lovers? Do we have sex with each other?" The image leaped into my mind, as it had that first day when I thought he was going to rape me, of Haunt's compact body pressed against mine, Haunt's clawed hands wandering across my breasts, my thighs, my belly. His rough scale-covered skin touching mine. His jutting muzzle seeking my lips. But of course there had been no rape when he came to my house and there had never been any kind of physical contact between us in our months of working together. It seemed almost unthinkable to me, the notion of having sexual relations with him or any other Ansaar. "How could you imagine such a thing?" I asked her.

"Everyone thinks that it's so."

"No—no, I swear—"

The woman acted as though she hadn't heard me. "You want to watch your step. It's one thing to work for them—we all have to do that. But loving them—oh, no, child, that will not be tolerated. Unwilling collaboration, yes. But fraternization, no. Do you understand me? What you've been doing simply will not be tolerated."

There was nothing I could say that would convince her of my innocence. She left me sitting there by myself, numb, bewildered, thinking, Ansaar whore! Ansaar whore!

When I saw Haunt later that day, I could not bear to tell him what the woman had said to me at lunch. It was too bizarre to share with him, and too shameful.

But I looked at him—that squat little Ansaar officer, with the scaly nonhuman skin and the purple birthmark and the long dangling arms and the short neck and the protruding jaws, and the prickly spines of his crest marching across the top of his head, and I thought, No, no, we could never be lovers. It would be too strange. There is too great a gap that must be crossed. But he is a decent person, a kindly person, and I feel no hatred for him despite the Annexation. For he sincerely thinks it was a good thing for Earth to become part of the Empire, that we can only benefit from what has happened.

And was I a traitor for dealing with him as I had done?

Yes. Yes, that I was. I saw that now, and it left me confused and sick. My eyes were open, finally. The Ansaar might not be villains, but they were conquerors, and we should not be allowing ourselves to do anything more for them than they made us do. I was no whore, certainly not; but in my naivete I had betrayed my people, and they hated me for it, and they were right to hate me as they did.

My life was in jeopardy, I knew.

If I went on working against my own kind, I would be made to suffer for it. For it was clear that the time of passive acceptance of the conquest was ending. After the first stunning shock of the Annexation, the people of Earth were beginning at last to contemplate striking back against their conquerors—and against those who had aided and abetted them.

Two days later, I was attacked again in the street.

It happened so swiftly that I never saw my attacker. Someone came darting out of the shadows, struck me hard across the face, and disappeared. I had never known such pain. The lip that had been cut in the first incident had been cut again, and it was as though a white-hot blade had been drawn across it.

"Tell me who it was," Haunt demanded. "A man? A woman? Give me any sort of clue—"

I shook my head. There was nothing I could tell him.

He sent out tracers anyway, hoping to turn up the existence of malcontents in the capital. He had me placed under the protection of security robots.

That only made things worse for me, of course. Now I never went anywhere without a robot bodyguard at my side; and wherever I went I was pointed at, hissed at, jeered at. Things were thrown at me from afar. The robot intercepted them, but it could not intercept the hatred that was aimed at me.

I decided that I would ask Haunt to release me from my personal annexation and send me back to my village. But something within me was unwilling, despite everything, to yield to the pressure I was feeling. I liked working for Haunt. I enjoyed helping him learn the history of Earth, because I was learning it too. And—this was the most complex part—I felt also that I was serving the cause of Earth by working with the Ansaar, because I was studying them while they were studying us, I was learning not only their language but their nature, and that might some day be useful in any attempt we might make to regain our independence.

Three indecisive days passed.

Then a tall white-haired man with chilly blue eyes halted me in the street outside Haunt's headquarters and said, "Do you recognize me, Laylah?"

I stared at him.

"No."

"Dain Italu is my name. I knew your father, years ago, in medical school. I met you five years ago, when I was traveling through your part of the country."

Five years. That was like an eternity to me. I shook my head and told him apologetically that I had no memory of our meeting.

"It makes no difference," he said. "Think of me as a friend, at any rate." He lowered his voice. "Do you know about the Partisans, Laylah?"

Partisans? The word meant nothing to me.

Quietly he said, "We work for Earth's freedom."

"I see."

"They tell me you're a traitor, Laylah. That you collaborate gladly with the Ansaar and that you even—" He broke off for a moment. "Well, there are more serious charges. It was proposed to sentence you to death. I spoke out for you, and said that I believed that no daughter of Tomas Walis could be guilty of the things with which you have been charged. I hope that I'm right, Laylah."

My face turned red and hot. "I'm not sleeping with an Ansaar, if that's what you were trying to say, Dr. Italu."

The Emperor and the Maula

"Well—"

"But I am working with one, yes. And studying him while he studies us." And I told him that I felt what I was learning about the Ansaar could be valuable to Earth's cause.

"Perhaps so," Italu said. "But you are in great danger, all the same. I warn you, Laylah: get yourself free from this Ansaar of yours. Stay away from him, have nothing further to do with him. Because otherwise—it could be very bad for you, Laylah—when the trouble starts—"

His expression was tense and strained, his voice had become ragged and uncertain. And it struck me suddenly that he was telling me something I probably should not be hearing—that out of whatever friendship had existed between him and my father he was going out of his way to warn me to distance myself from my Ansaar friend, because some uprising against the Ansaar was about to be launched, and I would be regarded as an enemy when it began.

He left me standing there, confused, deeply troubled.

I went upstairs to Haunt's office. He had an array of ancient documents spread out before him, historical texts going back to the era of warring nations.

"Look at these, Laylah," he said at once. "They've just been discovered in a buried vault. And they're fascinating—absolutely fascinating—but there are some things here I can't quite understand, and I've been waiting for you to arrive so that you could tell me—"

I have things to tell you, I thought. There's going to be a rebellion against the Annexation. You're at great risk, Haunt, and so am I.

But I said nothing about that. All morning long I looked at the documents with him, and I said nothing.

And that night, when the New Haraar uprising began in all its bloodiness—

Ah, Lordship, but morning has come again, I think! And so there is no more time for me to tell my tale!

⟫ 10.

THE EMPEROR said, "How sly you are, Laylah! You lead me along and lead me along, and then, just when I'm fully caught up in your story and eager to know what will happen next, you tell me that morning has come again! And so you stop."

"But morning has come again, Sire. I know that it has. And the executioner is waiting for me."

"Let him wait!" cried the Emperor. "Let him stew and fry! Who rules this Empire, tell me that—the High Ansaar of Haraar or the executioner? There is much that I need to hear from you. Secret partisans plotting rebellion—an insurrection against Ansaar rule—why am I learning of these things for the first time? Go on with your story. That night, when the New Haraar uprising began—"

"But I have talked all night, Sire. And there is so much more to tell; but not now, not now!" Laylah yawned delicately. "I beg your indulgence, for I must have some sleep now, Excellency. And you—the responsibilities of the throne await you. But tonight, when I resume—"

He smiled wryly.

"Tonight! Tonight! And so you buy yourself another day of life!"

"Ah, my lord, so I do, it seems. But it is life as a prisoner. What kind of life is that? I would gladly tell you everything in the next hour, and go at last to the fate that is reserved for me. But I am so tired now, Majesty. My eyes are red and swollen, and my voice—I can barely whisper, do you hear? So I suppose I must indeed live another day."

"Another day, yes. I will see you at sundown," said the Emperor Ryah VII, and Laylah was unable to tell whether his tone conveyed annoyance or amusement, or perhaps it was some of each. "Rest your voice, Laylah, and bathe your eyes. And prepare to bring your story to its conclusion this evening. Until then—"

And he was gone.

⫸ 11.

YOU HAVE ordered me, O Master of the Galaxy and Lord of All, to be concise in the telling of my tale. And so I will be; for I am a mere barbarian slave who may not refuse your command, and you are the Pillar of the Empire, upon whom all else depends, and how may I presume, O Majesty, to keep you further from the great tasks that are yours alone?

So let me tell you quickly of the things that happened on that terrible and violent evening in New Haraar, the administrative capital of Earth under the Annexation.

You would already know, if Earth were not so remote and insignificant a place, that Ansaar blood was shed that night. It surprises me that the incident is unknown to you, even so; for while Earth may be insignificant, the shedding of Ansaar blood by rebellious annexees surely is not. But of course this took place many years ago, during the reign of your illustrious father, and perhaps the episode has already receded into historical memory, the Empire being so huge and the number of occupied worlds so great—

But I see that I digress.

What happened was this:

You should know, O Highest of the High, that Earth is a planet with but a single moon, a large one that casts a brilliant gleam. This moon goes through its full complement of phases every twenty-eight of our days; and so a time comes once every twenty-eight days when no moonlight is seen, and the night sky is altogether dark except for the cool distant sparkle of the stars. It was on such a night, a night of no moon, when the Partisans struck their first blow against the soldiers of the Empire who had taken possession of our world.

It was a foolish and costly thing to do. It was insane. But you must remember, Excellency, that we were once a very violent race, who with great difficulty had suppressed the fury of our natures and taught ourselves the way of peace; but in the first dark days of the Annexation of Earth all the buried violence in our souls had come roaring back into us with the force and vehemence of a beast that had been chained too long. It was against each other, though, that we had turned first. We who had made ourselves so gentle and docile succeeded in reverting in a single night to the savage nature of our remote ancestors, and in our panic and terror during the hours of the Darkness and the Sound and the Voice we slew one another as if we were lost in a dream of ancient times. So it became clear to us that our warlike nature of old had not been cast off entirely, but merely had been put aside for a few hundred years; and now it was set loose again.

The Emperor and the Maula

This time, though, we turned our hands not against one another, but against our Ansaar masters.

There were two billions of us, and only a handful of Ansaar in the occupation force; and the Partisans reasoned that if they could pick a few Ansaar off, five here and ten there, the flame of resistance would catch and blaze high and we might eliminate them all in a matter of days; and then perhaps the Imperial Government would decide that we were too fierce, too difficult to govern, to be worth taking into the Empire.

It was insane, but at least it had been carefully planned. For weeks now the Partisans had been gathering weapons—not stolen Ansaar weapons, which were beyond our poor maula skills to understand, but the crude though effective weapons of Earth itself, rather—simple knives and clubs and such. A time of concerted attack was selected; and victims were picked, Ansaar whose movements could be predicted and who would very likely be in the streets when darkness fell on the next moonless night.

The hour of the uprising arrived; and the Partisans struck in the same instant in a dozen parts of New Haraar. With their knives, with their clubs, with their simple barbaric weapons.

Jjai Haunt was among those Ansaar who fell in that first onslaught.

If I had not needed to leave work early that night, I might well have been killed at his side. Or, perhaps, he would have been saved simply because he was with me, since the protective robot that went everywhere with me might have fended off the attackers as they came at us. But I had been suffering from some queasiness of the stomach all that day, and in early evening I asked permission to go home.

"As you wish," Haunt told me.

I still had said nothing to him of my conversation with Dain Italu. How could I? Haunt was my friend, yes; but to reveal the existence of the conspiracy was a deeper treason against my own kind than I could force myself to commit. Nor did I have any real evidence that there was any conspiracy—only the hints that I thought I had picked up in Dain Italu's words. So I kept silent; and thus I became implicated in the death of my friend. For which, O High Ansaar, I tell you I have felt great discomfort ever since. I will not pretend that I am without loyalty to my native world—quite the opposite, O High One, quite the opposite—but to allow a friend, whatever his race may be, to go to his death unwarned is a hard matter that sticks in your soul forever after. I was young, then, though, scarcely more than a child, an innocent girl unskilled in the ways of the world. It is the only excuse that I have to offer.

I hope Haunt's death was a swift one, at least.

They came out of the darkness as he left the building where he did his work. They surrounded him and struck him again and again; and though he fought back bravely—I know he did—there were too many, and their onslaught was too sudden, and they struck him down in the street and left him dying. Struck him with their knives and their clubs, with their simple barbaric weapons; and so they took the life of an Ansaar who had seen service on twenty worlds of the Empire.

Twelve other Ansaar died in that same moment in twelve different regions of New Haraar. The moonless night was lit by the red blaze of fifty fires. I heard the high whining of alarms, and from my window I saw Ansaar security robots gliding grimly through the streets.

Dain Italu came to me. "Get your things together, fast. There's no time to waste."

"What—where—?"

"Pack whatever you want to take with you, and let's get going. The Partisans will be here tonight to kill you."

I could do nothing better than stammer and blurt idiotic questions. Italu grabbed a little traveling case of mine, and threw a few things into it; and then I began to emerge from my stupor and collected a few things more—some clothing, a favorite book or two, a picture of my mother and father.

He rushed me down to the street. A floater was waiting there, an old model, perhaps older than I was. Italu thrust me into it and got into the driver's seat. I felt sick with fear. My stomach, queasy before all this had begun, was a knot of pain. There were angry shouts in the distance. The whole city seemed to be on fire around us.

"Where are you taking me?"

"To Sinon Kreish's castle," said Italu.

That astonished me. Sinon Kreish, Majesty, is dead now; but in his time he was said to be the wealthiest man on Earth—a merchant prince who lived in the kind of grandeur that only an Emperor can really understand. To me, to most of us, he was a legendary figure. This all was taking on the quality of a dream.

The floater came to life and rose almost vertically in the street. Within moments we were soaring high over the capital of the Ansaar occupation force. I could see fires raging in almost every quarter of the city.

"Have all the Ansaar been killed?" I asked.

"Only a few, Laylah. The ones who were marked for death."

I was silent a moment.

"And Procurator-Adjutant Haunt?"

"He was one of those who was marked," said Italu quietly.

That was hard. But not unexpected.

I said, after a time, "And I was marked for death too, then?"

"By a certain faction, yes. But another faction argued for saving you. You have been closer to the Ansaar than almost any of us, and you know them in a way that we will need later on. And so you are too valuable to be killed, Laylah. But emotions are running too high here tonight. I'm risking my own life by rescuing you, girl."

We were far from New Haraar by this time. Looking back, I saw the flames rising into the midnight sky.

I thought of Jjai Haunt lying dead on some street of the city. And I wanted to cry; but no tears would come. I was too frightened, too sick at heart, too bewildered.

I sat without speaking, arms clutched tight about my middle, as we soared onward toward my new life.

We must have been traveling east. For a little while everything about us was dark; but then, after scarcely any time at all, I saw pale brightness entering the sky ahead of us, and realized that we were heading into morning.

A great black mountain loomed before us.

"Mount Vorn," said Dain Italu. "The estate of Sinon Kreish."

The Emperor and the Maula

The floater swung low and swooped toward the landing stage of Sinon Kreish's Keep, on the black, craggy summit of Mount Vorn, one of Earth's loftiest mountains.

The floater doors opened and we stepped out. And instantly I knew that I had come to a place of wonders and miracles.

Golden sunlight ran in rivers across the iron-blue sky, dazzling me. It was warm here, even on this mountain-top, much warmer than in New Haraar. Sweet morning air rushed into my lungs like fine mellow wine, though I knew it had to be the scanty air of the heights. I tell you, Sire, there was magic in the air of Sinon Kreish's mountain. Ancient sorceries, floating dissolved in the fragrant atmosphere like flecks of gold in some rare elixir, penetrated my soul.

I looked around, astonished, dazed.

A woman of Sinon Kreish's staff had been waiting at the rim of the landing stage to greet us when we arrived; and now she moved toward us with wonderful grace, as though she was drifting weightless through the strange thin air.

"I am Kaivilda," she said. "You are welcome here, Laylah Walis. Come with me."

And I entered the dwelling of Sinon Kreish.

Kreish himself, O Master of All, was someone you might well have wished to know—a complex and sophisticated individual, wealthy and powerful and shrewd; a personage of grandeur and significance. Perceptive, influential, considerate, domineering, ruthless—all those terms would apply. I suggest in all respect, Sire, that an hour with him might have caused you to revise some of your notions of the barbaric qualities of the maulas of Earth.

And Sinon Kreish's castle on Mount Vorn would have been a fitting home even for an Emperor of the Ansaar. In the days that followed I wandered through it in an ecstasy of amazement. The life that was lived here was like nothing I had known in my little village beside the river.

The Keep had the look of a vast and gleaming onyx serpent, looping and leaping along the knifeblade-sharp ridge that is Mount Vorn's highest peak. The uppermost of its many levels, a transparent bubble of clearest quartz, contained Sinon Kreish's private bedchamber, with his conjuratorium just alongside. Below that—a horn-like excrescence of pure shining platinum boldly cantilevered out over the distant valley—was his trophy room and the chamber of his ancestral shrines; and just beside that, a blatant green eye of curving emerald, was the jutting hemisphere of his harmonic retreat.

A long white-vaulted passageway led at a steeply descending angle to the apartments of the members of Sinon Kreish's family. Access to these was guarded by a row of slender but effective blades, keen as razors, that would rise from the carnelian slabs of the passageway floor at the slightest provocation: the footfall of a mouse, let us say. A cascading series of balconies gave the inhabitants of these rooms access to the fresh mountain air and a view of the Plain of Oracles, where, so I was told, swarms of virtual realities cluster and hive.

A second passageway in the opposite direction opened into an elaborate pleasure-gallery supported by pillars of golden marble. Here the inhabitants of the castle could swim in a shimmering pool lined with garnet slabs, or suspend themselves in a column of warm air and permit streams of unquantified sensation to flood their sensory inputs, or put themselves in contact—through appropriate connectors and conduits—with the rhythms and sighing pulses of the cosmos. Here, also, Sinon Kreish maintained patterned rugs for focused meditation, banks of motile light-organisms for autohypnosis, a collection of stimulatory pistons and cartridges, and other devices whose purposes were unknown to me.

From there the structure made an undulating swaybacked curve and sent two wings back up the mountain at differing levels. One contained Sinon Kreish's collection of zoological marvels, the other his botanical garden. Between them, dangling in breathtaking verticality, were two levels of libraries and chambers for the housing of antiquities, bric-a-brac, and miscellaneous objets d'art. Centrally positioned between these rooms the castle's grand dining hall was appended, a single sturdy octagonal block of polished agate thrusting far out into the abyss.

The next level downward, the lowest of the series, was the room of social encounter, a cavernous hall where Sinon Kreish entertained the many guests that so frequently accepted his hospitality; appropriately lavish accommodations for those guests were located nearby. A landing stage for the convenience of these visitors' vehicles protruded from the mountain alongside. Behind it, hewn deep into the face of the mountain, were kitchens, waste-removal facilities, power-generation chambers, servants' quarters, and all the myriad other utilitarian rooms that served the castle's needs.

In this miraculous house I spent the next six months, cared for and cherished as though I were a member of Sinon Kreish's own family. Of Sinon Kreish himself I saw very little, naturally: an occasional glimpse of a striking and formidable figure, gaunt and towering, moving through the gleaming halls, and little more, at least in the beginning. But the others, his sons and daughters and more distant kin, treated me with love and warmth, and gradually I began to recover from the shocks and dark surprises of the period of the Annexation.

They are all dead now, O Lord of All, those sons and daughters and kin of Sinon Kreish, and the great castle itself was long ago reduced to rubble by the vengeful armies of the Ansaar. But the time of my stay in that wondrous place remains as bright as ever in my memory, and will forever.

There was no sense there of the Ansaar presence on Earth. The entire Annexation might never have taken place at all, so far as was apparent at the Keep. Everything there was as it had been before the conquest, nor did any Ansaar enter the place during the whole of my stay there. It was a long while before I learned why this was so.

In my first days there no one spoke to me about the Annexation, or my life in New Haraar, or any of the other troublesome events of recent months. I was treated the way any other guest might be, given a free run of the Keep, left to my own devices much of the time. It was purely a time of enjoyment and pleasure—a dream-life, Sire, a time out of time for me.

But gradually I was allowed to have some information about what was happening in the world beyond the precincts of this privileged castle.

The New Haraar uprising, I found out, had failed. Before dawn of that first night the Ansaar security forces had arrested nearly all of the conspirators and they had been taken away, no one knew where. Very likely they had all been executed, so it was thought. The Partisan movement had been crushed and the damaged buildings at the capital had all been repaired.

There had been terrible reprisals for the deaths of the thirteen Ansaar who had been killed during the insurrection. Some of Earth's greatest monuments had been levelled; several of our most productive agricultural zones had been sealed off and systematically ruined, so that next year's food supplies would have to be reduced everywhere; and word had gone out that any further attacks against Ansaar personnel would be met with even more serious measures. And so a truth was made clear to us which none of us in fact had ever doubted, O Supreme Omniscience: that the self-proclaimed benevolence of the Ansaar regime was nothing more than a veneer, that we were in fact slaves to our new masters, that if we were unruly we would be punished like beasts.

But why should we have expected anything else? Galactic empires are not founded on universal kindness.

In Sinon Kreish's castle, days and weeks went by, and each was very much like the others. I was never bored—it was impossible to know boredom, in a place of wonders like that—but I felt becalmed. Life took on a strangely static quality for me, for it seemed to be leading nowhere, containing no meaning. And then suddenly there was a great deal of meaning indeed.

I was told that Sinon Kreish had sent for me; and I was conducted through the levels of the castle to the master's private retreat, the emerald-walled globe at the very summit of the entire structure.

Soft mysterious sounds drifted through the air of that mysterious green realm, emanating, I suppose, from sonic crystals in the floor. Sinon Kreish stood in the center of the room, as rigid and upright as a tree, as I entered. It was the first time I had ever been alone with him, and I was frightened.

He said at once, "I will tell you a great secret, girl, that would be worth my life if ever it reached the ears of the Ansaar. I am the leader of the resistance movement here on Earth."

I looked at him in amazement. "The Partisans, you mean?"

He smiled. "Indirectly, yes. In the sense that their goal was to win back our planet's freedom, and that is my goal as well; and so I gave them a certain amount of aid for a time. But the Partisans were like wild beasts: they had no sense, no discretion. All they could think of was to murder, burn, destroy. What could that achieve, against the Ansaar? We murder ten of them and they kill ten thousand of us. We burn five of their buildings and they destroy five of our provinces." He smiled, and it was the fiercest, most icy smile I had ever seen. "No, no, no—the Partisans were all wrong, and they paid for their folly with their lives. The Empire is older and wiser and far stronger than we are; and it has dealt with rebels many times before. How many worlds, do you think, have ever won their freedom from the Ansaar, once they had been Annexed?"

I had no idea; and so I said nothing.

Sinon Kreish nodded, after a moment. "Correct. None. Not one, in the ninety thousand years of the Empire. There have been revolts, yes. There have been actual wars of independence. But not a single planet has ever escaped the Ansaar grasp for very long;

and the cost of the attempt has always been very high for those who have rebelled."

"Then we will be Ansaar slaves forever?" I asked.

"Perhaps we will. But I think not."

"If rebellion is impossible, then how—"

"We can never force the Ansaar to set us free, that I know. Never. But perhaps we can some day receive our freedom from them as a gift, do you see? Not if we resist them, girl, but if we freely and willingly cooperate with them. If we cooperate. It is the only way."

I was baffled. I understood nothing. Why would the Empire ever choose to relinquish its control over a meek and cooperative world? That was precisely the sort of world, was it not, that any empire would wish to absorb and retain. Sinon Kreish was speaking in bewildering paradoxes.

And he had called himself the leader of the resistance movement on Earth. Now he spoke of cooperation. How did one resist by cooperating?

He said, as though I had voiced my question aloud, "I deal with the Ansaar as I would with anyone with whom I am linked by common purpose. The Ansaar want us to be docile, manageable members of the Empire, and they will destroy us if we are not, though that is not what they would prefer; I want to avert the destruction of Earth just as they do, and so we have a common purpose, the Ansaar and I. Therefore I deal with them, do you see? And I am an advocate of peaceful cooperation. I launch no insurrections. I countenance no assassinations and no arson. Where I can, I prevent such things from happening."

Was he telling me that he had been instrumental in the downfall of the New Haraar Partisans? How many sides, I wondered, was this man on at once?

He peered down at me from his great height and said, "Enough of these airy abstractions, though. Let us get down to particulars, shall we, child? Dain Italu tells me that you speak the Ansaar language fluently and that you have made a special study of their ways and customs. Is this so?"

I nodded.

"Good."

"But I still have a great deal to learn," I said.

"Of course you do. And we want to give you the opportunity to learn it; for the more you know about the Ansaar, the more useful you will be."

Useful? To whom, I wondered? And how?

Sinon Kreish went on, "I have been speaking lately with my friend Antimon Felsert, who as you may know is the Ansaar High Procurator for Earth."

His friend? The word took my breath away.

"The High Procurator," said Sinon Kreish, "is willing to allow a small group of young people from Earth to be sent abroad into the Empire to study Imperial ways. I have convinced him, you see, that mankind can never be properly integrated into the Empire of which it has so abruptly become a part without a proper knowledge of the society that it is joining." He smiled. "We have been so isolated, of course—so remote from the main currents of galactic life. But if a few of our bright young folk are permitted to go forth into the Empire to travel and study, they can ultimately serve as interpreters between the races, do you see? They can explain the ways of the Ansaar to the people of Earth, and they can help the Ansaar learn something of our ways as well. It would be an extension of what you were doing when you were working with Procurator-Adjutant Haunt, essentially. A considerable extension."

I looked up at him, wide-eyed with shock.

"You're turning me over to the Ansaar? I'm going to leave Earth?"

"Only if you are willing, of course. Are you willing?"

I was thunderstruck. This was all so sudden. I searched desperately for words.

"Well—yes—I think—that is—"

"You understand that there would be no possibility of your ever setting foot on the core worlds of the Empire, of course, the ones inhabited by the Ansaar themselves, the worlds of so-called Imperial Space. Entry to those is forbidden to all maulas. —You know what the word maula means, do you?"

Reddening, I said, "Yes. Barbarian."

"The translation is a little extreme. The word actually refers simply to those who have not yet reached a certain stage in the development of civilization. But, yes, I suppose you could say 'barbarian' is basically what they mean by it. As a maula, you could never enter Imperial Space, but that still leaves the immense region known as Territorial Space, which is populated largely by non-Ansaar races that have moved beyond maula status but are nevertheless not yet entitled to full Imperial citizenship. There are large Ansaar populations on all the Territorial worlds, however. You will have ample subjects for your studies. If indeed you are willing to undertake such a venture. You have not yet said that you are."

"Well—"

"Tell me yes or tell me no," he said, his eyes flashing now with irritation.

"Yes," I declared. "Yes, yes, of course! Of course I'll go!"

He smiled, somewhat bleakly. "Good. I was certain you would not refuse to perform this service for your race."

Service?

I was still mystified. What service was Sinon Kreish asking me to perform?

But I did not dare speak up. It was sufficient that I would be given an opportunity to go out into the galaxy. I had found the path that I wanted to follow at last—the path of knowledge, of study—and what I wanted to study, more than anything else, was the unimaginable richness and complexity of the vast Empire that had so casually swallowed up my native world. Here was Sinon Kreish offering me the key to the galaxy. I would be a fool not to snatch it from him.

And so it was all agreed; and a day or two later I left the castle of Sinon Kreish and traveled back across the world to the city of New Haraar. Where, to my utter astonishment, I soon found myself being ushered into the presence of Antimon Felsert, the High Procurator for Earth.

—But I think that morning has come again, Sire. My time is at an end, and I must cease telling my tale.

▷▷ 12.

"THIS ANTIMON Felsert," said the Emperor. "His name seems familiar to me."

"It is morning, Sire!"

"Yes, yes, I know," the Emperor said, with an edge of impatience on his voice. "Felsert, Felsert—"

"He was assassinated by terrorists," said Laylah. "In the last year of your father's reign. Sinon Kreish was accused of having organized the plot, and he and his entire family were put to death, and their castle destroyed. But I doubt very much that he had any part in it. As I've just told you, he had no faith in the use of violent means against the occupying forces."

"Yes," the Emperor said, half to himself. "The Felsert assassination. I remember now. The first High Procurator to be killed by natives in something like four thousand years. There were severe worldwide reprisals, weren't there? Other than the Sinon Kreish execution."

"Extremely severe, Sire, so I understand. I was far from Earth at the time, myself—I was living on one of the Bessiral worlds then—but I know that my world was made to suffer heavily for High Procurator Felsert's death. I was deeply shocked, myself, Majesty. By the reprisals, of course—but also by the assassination. It seemed a pointless thing to me. And I had great respect for High Procurator Felsert."

"Indeed. Indeed."

The Emperor seemed oddly unwilling to leave.

Laylah said again, "Is it not morning, Sire?"

The Emperor, who had wandered to the far side of the room, swung around and glared at her. In exasperation he cried, "It is morning, yes."

"And the executioner—"

"The executioner, the executioner, the executioner! Vipraint the executioner! Kiplaa him! Why are you in such a hurry to die, woman?"

"You misunderstand me, Majesty. I'm not in any hurry at all. But the law requires—"

"Do you presume to teach me the law?" cried the Emperor Ryah.

"A thousand pardons, Sire. I was only reminding you—"

"Yes. Yes. Yes. Yes."

"But if in your great mercy, All-Powerful, you choose to let this poor maula remain alive another day, I would offer thanks to the gods of all the worlds."

Sourly the Emperor said, "I asked you to tell me why you had come to Haraar even though you knew it would mean your death to do so. You responded by telling me the story of the Annexation

The Emperor and the Maula

of Earth. I asked you for details of what appeared to have been your rape at the hands of an Ansaar soldier, and you responded by telling me that there had been no rape, that the Ansaar had come to you to ask for your help, and that he became your friend and protector. I asked you to tell me the details of the conspiracy that cost your Ansaar friend his life, and you responded with an account of your visit to the gaudy castle of some rich Earthman who eventually was found guilty of treason against the Empire. Three nights have passed in this story-telling, and I have come to know a great deal now about who you are and what you have experienced, and yet I have had no proper answers yet to any of my questions. And all the while, the desecration of our holy world that you have committed continues to cry out for punishment. What am I to do with you, Laylah Walis? What am I to do with you?"

"You are the Guardian of the Law, Majesty. You are free at any time to deliver me up to those who carry out its precepts."

"But I want answers from you first!"

"Even so, even so. Come to me again tonight, and I will try to tell you all that you desire to know. But surely you must not stay here any longer this morning. The duties of the court—"

"Yes, the duties of the court," said the Emperor quietly. "The duties of the court! Who has any concept, I often ask, of what the duties of the court are like? No wonder my father wept bright red tears for me when my brother fled to the monastery and the crown became destined for me! The duties of the court!" His voice had begun to rise. With visible effort he brought it under control. "Today, Laylah: the Twelve Despots of Geeziyangiyang arrive in the third hour, and it will take them two hours more simply to work out the order of precedence in which they want to pay their courtesies to me. And then—the trade delegation of Gimmil-Gib-Huish, with a gift of who knows what for the Imperial Zoological Gardens: poisonous serpents, most likely. But they have to be thanked. Afterward the League of the Fertile Womb, presenting this year's winner of the Imperial Order of the Crystal Egg. Then the Guild of Prophets, with the annual predictions—the champion verbish-breeder of Zabor Province, to receive her medal—the Imperial Architect, to complain about the modifications that I've requested for the Pavilion of the Grand Celestial Viewing—and then—then—it never ends, do you realize that? What's the point of having absolute power, if you fritter it away on a million ceremonial audiences a day? Lord of All! Master of the Universe!" The Emperor laughed wildly. Then, his voice quieter again, almost eerily contained, he said, "The duties of the court, as you say, must not be shirked. Ah, but if I could! If I only could! Thraak the duties of the court! Gedoy the duties of the court! Impossible. Impossible. I'll go now. I'll return at sundown." He crossed the room, and stood studying her for a moment or two at close range; and then his hand reached out—his claws, Laylah noticed for the first time, were elegantly trimmed and rounded—and he lightly touched the curve of her jaw, running his hand up almost to her ear in a gesture that seemed to be one of tenderness. In an oddly soft voice he said, "How fascinating you are! And how maddening. Until later, then, Laylah."

And once more he was gone.

▷▷ 13.

AJESTY—LIGHT OF the Cosmos—Supreme Monarch of the Million Suns—

If I may resume—

I was brought into the presence of the High Procurator for Earth, Antimon Felsert, in his office atop the highest tower of the city of New Haraar.

Never before had I beheld an Ansaar even of the middle castes. I did not even have a clear understanding of the Ansaar castes then. It had seemed to me that Procurator-Adjutant Haunt must surely come from an important Ansaar level; but he, of course, was a man of one of the lower castes who had risen into authority by virtue of long service, high ability, and the fact that caste structures are not as rigidly observed on newly annexed worlds as they are in the heartland of the Empire. I knew none of that yet.

But I could see at once, when I stood before High Procurator Felsert, that he was different from other Ansaar. I saw it in the color of his skin, the shape and size of his crest, the proportions of his limbs. He differed as much in appearance from Jjai Haunt and the other Ansaar I had seen as—no, forgive me, Majesty, I am in error; for I was about to say that the gulf between Felsert and Haunt was roughly the same as the gulf that separates an Ansaar of the Imperial caste from a mid-caste Ansaar. But that is not true. To an undiscriminating human eye Felsert and Haunt would not have looked very different from each other at all. The Imperial caste is a caste unto itself.

My eye was becoming discriminating, though. That is the point I meant to introduce.

High Procurator Felsert looked me over with some mild interest and said, in excellent English, "So you're the girl that Sinon Kreish has sent us for the study program. The one who used to work with Jjai Haunt. How old are you, girl?"

"Sixteen," I said. "Almost seventeen."

"A great loss, Haunt. One of our best researchers. I have his report here on you. —Do you speak Universal Imperial, girl?"

"I do."

"And can you read it?"

"Yes, sir."

"Here, then. Glance through this."

He tossed me a small, glossy yellow cube: a memorandum cube, of course, but it was the first one I had ever seen. I held it in my hand, frowning, until High Procurator Felsert told me in somewhat curt tones how to activate it. I found the stud and turned it and Jjai Haunt's report on me materialized in bright red letters in the air in front of me.

...intelligent, eager to please...a fast learner...almost suspiciously trustworthy...perhaps somewhat immature for her age, considering that human females are capable of reproduction by the time they have lived twelve or thirteen years...

"What do you think he meant, 'almost suspiciously trustworthy'?" High Procurator Felsert asked me, speaking now in Universal Imperial.

"I have no idea, sir." I made my reply in the same language.

"And 'eager to please.' Why would you be eager to please an Ansaar?"

"You are our masters," I said simply.

"Reason enough to hate us, then."

"I have never hated anyone, sir. It seems a waste of emotional energy."

High Procurator Felsert laughed. The Ansaar way of laughing is nothing like our own, of course, but I knew by now that the sound he had made indicated amusement.

He asked me a few questions more. It was clear to me that they were only routine, that all the necessary decisions concerning my fate had already been made.

And indeed, within hours after the High Procurator had dismissed me from his office, I was told to make myself ready for departure from Earth. My long years of exploration and study were about to begin.

And there is so much for me to tell you about those years!

I know you want me to be concise, O Prince of Princes and Master of the Stars. But it was a journey of eighteen years for me, from Earth to this holy world of Haraar and the presence of your majestic self, and how can I sum up those eighteen years in only a few words? The Empire is immense, and I have seen much of it; and everything that happened to me in those eighteen years was an essential event in the shaping of the path that brought me finally to the palace of the Most Holy Defender of the Race.

Let me explain, Sire.

There were nineteen of us in the first group of humans to be sent to the Territories: twelve men, seven women. The youngest of us was fifteen and the oldest nearly forty. Included among us were poets, scholars, scientists, some of the finest minds Earth possessed. I felt very young and very insignificant among them, during the six weeks of our briefing period, when we were taught something of the reach and spread of the Empire into which we shortly would be thrust.

Then we were sent forth, in groups of three or four, to different worlds of the Ansaar Territories.

I went to Bethareth, first, in the Hklplod system: a golden world of a golden sun, where sleek beautiful creatures, limbless like serpents, worship a monster-god that dwells atop a great mountain. I lived among them for a year, and made the pilgrimage to the mountain-top with them, and watched them as they pressed their jewel-studded foreheads against the stone flank of their god. From there I went to Giallo Giallo of the Mirilores, a world of eternal snows and frozen oceans, and traveled with Ansaar explorers into an underground realm of torrid caverns and turbulent lava rivers, a realm so strange that it would take me six of these nights simply to describe what I saw there.

The Emperor and the Maula

And then to Sepulmideine, the World of Chained Moons, where the sky burns with fragrant fires—to Mikkalthrom, where the Emperor Gorn XIX lies buried in a stasis tomb that will not open for fifty thousand Imperial years—to Gambelimeli-dinul, the pleasure-world of the Eastern Territories—

Oh, Majesty, Majesty, how can I tell you the things I have seen? For there was so much, so very much! From world to world I went, and each world held more than one could see in a dozen lifetimes; and yet I knew that this was only the edge of the edge of the Empire's myriad Territories, that I could travel on and on forever and not embrace the whole Ansaar universe, or even just the part of it that maulas are permitted to enter.

The first years of my travels were wondrous beyond words. The entire cosmos lay open to me.

The highest moment of those years—and the darkest—came for me on a world called Vulcri, a red world of the red sun Kiteil, as I stood by the shores of the lake of Costa Stambool, staring at the ruins of the city of the same name that had been the capital of an empire which had risen and fallen long before the first Ansaar had ever gone forth from Haraar—

It was all there, layer upon jumbled layer. The crooked streets of the oldest levels, rooted in the dying days of an era called the Second Mandala and contemptuously built upon by the glorious successors of that impoverished civilization: the clumsy primitive walls and foundations were hidden beneath the accretions of a thousand later centuries, and yet they glowed with an insistent scarlet phosphorescence, defiantly proclaiming their former significance even in this overwhelmed condition. Above them were the chalcedony halls of the Concord of Worlds, and above those sat the streets of the City of Brass, and sprawling over those were the remains of the slopes and slideways of gaudy Glissade, the pleasure-suburb of Later Costa Stambool. I was able to see it all at once, every phase of that ancient capital city's long history. Every layer showed the marks of its destruction at the hands of subsequent improvers of the city and over everything else was brutally superimposed the final scars that were inflicted by the vandals who ushered in the climactic Fourth Mandala of Costa Stambool with fire and the sword.

Here were the palaces of obsolete dynasties and the temples of forgotten gods; here were shops that dealt in treasures that were already incalculably ancient when the Ansaar were young, and taverns peddling vintages that have long turned to dust, and parks green with trees and shrubs of species no longer known to the universe. A great marble slab proclaimed in an undecipherable language the glories of an empire that spanned ten solar systems but whose name and those of all its monarchs are lost beyond retrieval. And here were the gouges and slashes of the warriors of the Fourth Mandala, cutting across everything, shouting of mortality. There was no end to the spectacle.

What I saw was marvelous, marvelous. I stood stock-still, letting the glories of this ancient civilization flood through my stunned soul. My mind, filled with the pre-programmed data of my guide, roved from layer to layer, from epoch to epoch. This was the palace of the Triple Queen, and this was the courtyard of the Emperor of All, and these identical marble structures were the cells in which the Tribunal of the People, that fifty-minded entity which had governed here for thirty centuries of grimly imposed harmony, lived chin-deep in pools of luminous nutrients drawn from the dissolved bodies of their citizenry. I saw the celebrated Library of Old Stambool, where books in the form of many-faceted gems, containing in their rigid lattices every word that had ever been written, spilled from iron-bound chests. I peered into the Gymnasium and it seemed to me that a howling triple-headed beast in fetters glared back at me from the Field of Combat with fiery eyes. I entered the Market of All Wonders, where amazing merchandise of a thousand worlds once was laid out in open arcades, everything free for the taking, gift of They-Who-Provide, loving guardians of this greatest of all cities. I had never seen anything like it; I had never so much as imagined anything like it.

I was numb with a surfeit of miracle. I stood in silence for what felt like hours, gazing out over the immense ruins of Costa Stambool.

Then a voice by my side said, "Some day, perhaps, the capital of the Ansaar will be a ruin like this, eh?"

The sacrilegious words astounded me. I whirled; and saw that a man—a human!—had quietly come upon me out of somewhere while I still stood in that trance of wonder. He was smiling at me in an oddly familiar way.

"Are you shocked, Laylah?" he asked me.

"How do you know my name?"

He laughed. "You don't recognize me, do you?"

I looked—looked—

The eyes. The shape of the lips. The curve of the smile.

"Vann?" I said, hesitantly.

"Who else, Laylah! Your long-lost brother Vann! Who comes walking right up to you at the edge of nowhere and says hello! Can you believe it, Laylah? Two needles, we are, in a haystack a million light-years across!"

He had been a boy when I had last seen him. And now—

We fell into each other's arms, laughing and crying, there beside the ruins of lost Costa Stambool.

I have never known a more wonderful moment, Sire, in my life. But it turned to ashes almost at once. For as we walked back toward the visitor lodge, Vann and I, babbling to each other of all that had happened us since the day of the Darkness and the Sound and the Voice, he said something suddenly to me that brought me up short with horror and fright, something so dark and mad that I knew then that I had found and lost him at one and the same time. For what he said, Majesty, was utter treason. What my brother said to me, there amid all the strangeness of Costa Stambool on the planet called Vulcri—

Ah, but the time has come for me to halt for tonight, eh, Majesty? I have used up so many hours in my descriptions of wonders that I will have to tell you tomorrow of my brother's words, and the effect they had on me, and what happened afterward. Is that not so, Majesty? Is that not so? And so you must spare my life for one more day, if you will. What shall it be, Majesty? The executioner's block for me, or another day and a night of life? For the decision is yours, O Master of All, O Lord of the Universe.

▷▷ 14.

THE EMPEROR was smiling.

"You won't ever finish the story, will you, Laylah? You'll go on spinning it out for a hundred years, and then a hundred years more, if I allow it. Tell me: am I wrong?"

"There is so much to tell, Majesty!"

"Yes, and you will insist on telling it all. Whereas all I wanted to know from you was—well, you know what I wanted to find out. Simply why you had risked coming to Haraar, when you knew that you would die for it." He shook his head. "And instead you tell me this, you tell me that, you tell me one thing after another—"

"It is all part of the story, Majesty. Everything is linked to everything else. But I do confess that I have been in no hurry to reach the conclusion. If you will grant me one more night, or perhaps two, perhaps then I would be able to—" She glanced sharply at him. "Or if I have begun to bore you, perhaps we should stop for good right here. The executioner's patience was exhausted long ago; and now, I think, yours is also. Very well. I will prolong the story no longer. My tale is over. I bid you farewell forever, Majesty. May you reign and prosper for seven times seven thousand years." And she began to make the Ansaar sign of blessing, that is made only by those who are about to die.

The Emperor caught her hand in mid-gesture and brought it back down to her side.

"No," he said.

"No?"

"There'll be no executions today. And there'll be more story-telling tonight. But promise me one thing, Laylah!"

"That I finish it this evening?"

"Yes. Yes. Yes."

She bowed and made the sweeping gesture of submission.

"I will do my best, Majesty. Though it costs me my life, and I know that it will, tonight will see the last of my story. That much I promise you with all my heart, O Light of the Cosmos—O Supreme Monarch of the Million Suns—"

> Bogan 27, 82nd Dynastic Cycle
> (August 15—I think—A.D. 3001)
> I have him! He's caught good and proper, that much is certain! And he will sit and listen to me—and sit—and listen—as long as I want him to—as long as I need him to—
>
> —From the Diaries of Laylah Walis

▷▷ 15.

UT THIS was the night of nights, and she could not bring herself to begin.

"Tonight," the Emperor prompted at last, "You said you would tell me what your brother said to you at Costa Stambool, and what effect it had on you."

"Yes." And still she hesitated, for this was the most difficult moment of all. Everything she meant to say tonight had been arranged properly in her mind, but now, suddenly, for the first time since her arrival, words would not come.

Again he spoke into her silence: "Let me say it for you. What he told you was that he was a key member of the anti-Imperial resistance, that he knew you were expert in Ansaar language and customs, and that he had come to you to ask you to make the journey to Haraar, inveigle yourself into my palace, win my affection with your extraordinary charm...and assassinate me."

He said it quietly, but his words struck her like hammerblows. She sat frozen, stunned, lost in a maelstrom of panic.

"Is this not so, Laylah?" He was smiling. "Speak. Or have you lost your voice?"

Hoarsely she replied, "These are the things I meant to tell you tonight, yes. But how is it you know them already?"

"From your diary, of course."

"My diary? How could you read my diary? My diary is in English!"

"Which is the main language of Earth. And Earth is a world of the Empire." His tone remained gentle. He was not speaking as an Emperor might speak. "Do you think we'd annex a world and not learn its language? While you were asleep an expert in your language entered and read your little book. —But tell me, Laylah: *Would* you assassinate me?"

"No. Never. Never!" She was trembling. She could barely get the words out.

"I believe you," he said, and he sounded sincere. "Yet that is what you came to Haraar to do. Is it because you find me so fascinating? Because you have fallen in love with me?" He was playing with her, again, the lion toying with his prey. "Or because you have come to see the uselessness of killing me?"

"All of that," she said. Some strength returned to her voice. "Killing you would have been pointless. The Empire has survived the deaths of hundreds of Emperors, and will go on and on regardless of who is on the throne. —But why should we discuss this? The game is over, Majesty. Summon your executioner."

"Not just yet. The other part, first: have you really fallen in love with me? With the arch-enemy of your people?"

His gaze grew fierce. She could not meet his eyes.

"I admit being fascinated by you. That's not quite the same thing as love."

"Agreed. I feel a fascination too. You know that, don't you? Why else do I listen to you, night after night, when I have so much else to do? The lovely maula who risks her life to come to Haraar—who talks her way right into the Emperor's presence—who tells him tales of her world that hold him helpless night after night—"

"I played a dangerous game, and I lost." The trembling had stopped. She felt very calm. "Shall we end this little session now? I no longer wish to prolong our conversations."

"But I do, Laylah. —What if I were to offer you Earth's freedom from Ansaar rule?"

She gasped. Once again he had caught her unawares and sent her reeling. "Earth's—freedom—?"

"As an autonomous member of the Empire. An end to Ansaar occupation, and freedom for its citizens to travel in Imperial Space. Such a thing is within my power to grant. I saw these lines in your diary, too, from one of your ancient poets: *Titles are shadows, crowns are empty things; the good of subjects is the end of kings.* So I believe, Laylah: the good of subjects. I am no tyrant, you know. I will set your little world free."

"This is an ugly joke. It's cruel of you to trifle with me like this."

"I'm neither joking nor trifling. The freedom of Earth is yours, Laylah." And, after a moment: "As a wedding gift, that is." His Ansaar hand reached for hers. "'I would gladly go on speaking with him forever,' you wrote. The opportunity is yours. You fascinate me to the point of love, Laylah. I invite you to become one of my Cherished Major Wives."

When she could speak again she said, "One of how many, may I ask?"

"You would be the sixth."

"Ah. The sixth." She was past the first rush of astonishment, almost calm, now. But not the Emperor. His eyes were retracted in tension, the vertical pupil-slits barely in view. "Cherished Wife Number Six! What a strange fate for a quiet girl from Earth!" She mused on it while he stared tautly, knotting and unknotting his fingers. "Well, we can discuss it, Majesty. Yes. We can discuss it, I suppose, in the days ahead."

He nodded. "By all means. We can discuss it. I will come to you as before, and you will tell me your tales, and perhaps, by and by—"

"By and by," she said. "Yes. Perhaps."

She forced herself to maintain her eerie calmness, for other wise she would break loose entirely from her moorings.

Sixth Cherished Wife! And Earth an autonomous world! Yes, but could she? Would she? By and by, perhaps. Perhaps. By and by.

"Tell me the next story, Laylah."

▷ ◁

Very well. I must tell you, then, Majesty, that from Costa Stambool I went onward to the forbidden world of Grand Binella, the planet of the Oracle Plain, of which they say that in its shapes and colors are the answers to all the questions that have ever been asked and many that have not yet been framed. Near the Plain are the mountains called the Angelon, where one walks on a carpet of rubies and emeralds. Farther on—almost at the horizon—one sees a body of motionless black water, the Sea of Miaule, with Sapont Island smoldering just off shore, a place of demons and basilisks.

I made my way to this terrifying world, Sire, at my brother's suggestion, because he felt that among those demons and basilisks I might learn certain useful things, things that would stand me in good stead if ever I found myself in the place where I find myself now. And so, upon my arrival there—